PUFFIN BOOKS
Editor: Kaye Webb

HORSE IN THE HOUSE

Melanie Webb was one of those girls who can't live without a horse. She wouldn't have minded if it had been a scrubby little pony, so long as she had one, but the horse she had was a winner, a white palomino stallion called Orbit.

Orbit had been given to Melanie when she was ten and he was only three months old, and they had been growing up together ever since. Orbit was never out of her thoughts, and he waited all day for the moment she came home from school to ride him.

Then Mom and Pop went away to San Francisco for a week, giving Melanie the perfect opportunity to put her cherished plan into action – her secret wish to bring Orbit inside the house. And any worries she had about the suspicious horse-dealer who had been haunting the neighbourhood were pushed to the back of her mind.

Then one night Melanie went out to the barn to say good night to Orbit. But when she got there, there was no one to say it to. Orbit was gone, and the unoccupied stable was intolerably desolate and empty.

Melanie felt useless, like a captain without a ship. Yet some-where, *somewhere* in this nightmarish world, Orbit existed. And somewhere, she was sure of it, locked in her head was some little memory, a shred of a clue to the thief.

For readers of ten upwards, especially girls.

Cover design by Jennifer Taggart

WILLIAM CORBIN

Horse in the House

ILLUSTRATED BY
SAM SAVITT

PUFFIN BOOKS

Puffin Books, Penguin Books Ltd, Harmondsworth, Middlesex, England
Penguin Books Australia Ltd, Ringwood, Victoria, Australia
Penguin Books (N.Z.) Ltd, 182–190 Wairau Road, Auckland 10, New Zealand

—

First published in the U.S.A. 1964
Published in Great Britain by Methuen 1966
Published in Puffin Books 1969
Reprinted 1971, 1973, 1975
Copyright © William McGraw, 1964

—

Made and printed in Great Britain by
Cox & Wyman Ltd, London, Reading and Fakenham
Set in Intertype Plantin

Chapter 1

THE town of Cascade, Oregon, was not so small that the presence of a stranger would attract undue attention.

At the moment, certainly, the heavy-shouldered, youngish man in battered cowboy boots who sat hunched at the corner of the Cascade Shake Shop was getting no attention at all from the noisy after-school-on-Friday crowd at the long table behind him.

Nor did the stranger, stolidly chewing his way through a slab of pie, give any indication that he was aware the young people existed. Not, that is, until one strong voice suddenly carried above the babble of the others.

'Oh yes she will! If Melanie Webb says she's going to keep her horse in the house, that's exactly what she's going to do!'

The babble rose up, drowning whatever else the lone speaker might have been saying, and the stranger at the counter sat motionless as a stone. His jaws had stopped moving the instant the name Melanie Webb had been spoken. Then he turned slowly on the counter stool and surveyed the group at the table with an air of casual indifference.

5

A few minutes later, when the noisy group had gone out, still hotly arguing, he got up and began rolling a cigarette. In the process he moved over to the littered table just vacated and picked up a sheet of paper left there by a girl who had been waving it around while she talked.

Outside, he leaned against a telephone pole and scanned the sheet, moving his lips as he read.

Blurrily mimeographed in purple ink, the sheet proclaimed itself to be *The Cascadian* – Cascade School's Monthly News-letter – Conrad Wemmer Editor-in-Chief. After a minute he found what he was looking for – the name, in capital letters, of Melanie Webb. It was halfway down a list of names on the reverse side of the sheet under the heading *Summer Madness* – a list which informed the reader that each member of the eighth grade graduating class was herewith disclosing what he or she was going to do with the vacation that lay ahead.

The stranger read only what came after the name he had been looking for: 'I'm going to teach my horse to live in the house so he can civilize my sisters.'

Raising his eyes, the man squinted with the effort of thought. Then, with sudden purposefulness, he strode quickly to the phone booth on the corner.

'It's me, Joe,' he said when he got his number. 'Listen, about this Webb kid. I just latched on to a new angle. Changes our whole approach. Now here's what you got to do . . .'

He spent five minutes telling the person named Joe what to do and ended with, 'Got it straight? Okay. See you Monday.' With his broad, sweat-stained hat tilted back on his head, he strolled away with the air of a man who has done a good day's work.

The only good thing about Monday, for Melanie Webb, was the fact that it was her last Monday at Cascade School. Apart from that, it was a ghastly day – an 'absolutely *scabrous* day', as her sister Katie would have put it.

For this she had the exasperating Conrad Wemmer to thank

6

– Conrad and his stupid ideas about what people wanted to read in a school paper. Of course, to be truthful she had herself to thank, too. If she hadn't given in to an impulse born of annoyance at Conrad and his silly questionnaire about summer-time plans, she wouldn't now be having to spend the last Monday of the school year enduring the unfunny jokes of her classmates.

The questionnaire had made the rounds one day nearly two weeks before, and the very sight of it, like the sight of Conrad himself, had as usual brought out the worst in Melanie. To her, Conrad and questionnaires went together like sulphur and molasses, chills and fever, or famine and pestilence.

'*The Good Ol' Summer Time*' was its heading. Conrad imprisoned almost all his published utterances in quotation marks.

'*Fellow Cascadians:* Three months of "freedom" are almost upon us. For our last "big issue" of the "school year" the staff of *The Cascadian* wants to print how each and every one of you is going to spend his "well-earned" (hah hah) vacation. Just fill out the blank after your name.'

Melanie could just as easily have written something dull and sensible, as everybody else did, and ordinarily she might have done so. But she didn't. In her exasperated mood, nothing but some outrageous remark would do. So she wrote the first thing that came into her head, passed the questionnaire along, and promptly forgot about it.

Now she was paying for her impulsiveness. Conrad's newsletter had been distributed at the end of last period on Friday, and everybody in school had had a whole week-end in which to think up something witty to say to Melanie about the horse in her house. The strain of being a good sport for several hours would have tried the patience of a far more saintly girl than she; and when the final buzzer sounded she dashed for the school bus.

Just three miles away from the school from which Melanie

7

Webb was escaping, a palomino stallion in a pasture as green as springtime itself suddenly raised his silky muzzle from the grass between his white-stockinged forelegs. Something had occurred to remind him that the lazy day was getting along, and that very soon now things would begin to happen. He did a dancing half turn to face the south-east corner of the pasture, flicked his ears forward to listen, and stood as still as a statue. The May sun glinted on the polished copper of his winter coat, which would turn by August to a creamy gold. Nothing about him moved but his ever-questing nostrils and those few wisps of his sweeping, nearly white mane and tail that could be stirred by an experimental sort of breeze.

The name of this living statue, according to the registry papers in a picture-frame on the wall of Melanie's room, was Star-Wanderer. He was, the papers said, 'by Astronaut, out of Galaxie'.

Melanie, after due deliberation, had condensed the whole celestial mouthful into a manageable name. She had named him, simply, Orbit.

That impromptu christening had taken place four years ago when Melanie was ten years old and Orbit was three months. They had been growing up together ever since – a rather one-sided affair, because in that time Melanie had gained only thirty-two pounds to Orbit's seven hundred. These statistics were completely unimportant, however, because no matter how big Orbit grew Melanie always felt a little bigger. Obviously he felt that way, too.

He of course had no recollection of the day and the way they met. Melanie, on the other hand, could remember all too clearly. It was a dreadful, nightmarish way, and she seldom thought about it any more. Mercifully so.

Everything that led up to it had begun long ago. For no reason anyone could put a name to, Melanie had been one of those little girls who come along often enough to add up to an astonishing number, little girls who seem to have been born with a love of anything that goes by the name of horseflesh.

Little girls who are utterly certain by the age of five that if they can't have some horsy creature of their own – anything at all from a scrubby pony to a racing thoroughbred – they will quite literally die.

Melanie's father had reached the same conclusion – or said he had. Not even Melanie could always tell whether Pop was serious or not. At any rate, when she was eight Pop had sold the house in Portland and bought the fifteen-acre place they had lived on ever since. Along with it had come Gigi, the little Shetland mare.

If Melanie lived forever she would never forget the day of the move when Pop took her hand and, with a wink at Mom, led her down to the small, neat barn painted yellow and grey to match the house. On the way, he said, 'With the place and all, I didn't have money enough left to buy a *big* horse, but maybe a little one will do for now.' He had thrown open the door to the big box stall then – there was Gigi, the answer to every dream and prayer of Melanie's short lifetime.

After a while, when he could get a word in, he had said, very soberly, 'She's yours, Mellie-girl.' Pop was the only one who ever called her that. 'She's all yours, but that means you're part hers, too. She has the right to expect of you what you expect of me, which is to be kept fed, and well, and safe.'

Two years later, when the terrible nightmare time came, she would have given everything she owned, or hoped to own, to have been able to forget those words. Dusk had come early that October night. They were just finishing dinner – she and her older sisters, and Mom and Pop, of course. Pop's coffee cup was halfway to his lips when suddenly there came the squeal of skidding tyres on the road outside. A man's voice rose in a muffled shout. Then the scream. It was almost human – like a woman's scream, but not enough like one to deceive Melanie; and in that moment her mind leaped to sickening recollection. Not only had she failed to fasten the barn door after feeding Gigi, she had left open the gate to the lane as well – the lane that led past the house and down to the road.

9

Pop's cup clattered into the saucer and the whole table leaped as he lunged to his feet. Melanie found herself on her feet, too, a strange sobbing noise tearing its way painfully up through her throat. Then she whirled and would have run for the front door but Pop moved swiftly and his big hand closed tightly around her arm, nearly lifting her off her feet.

'Go to your room! Go. You hear?' He rapped out the words in a harsh voice she had never heard before.

'Sally, see that she goes,' he told Melanie's mother. 'Stay with her. You! Girls! One of you turn on the radio. Loud. And leave it that way.' His feet pounded through the living-room and the door slammed behind him.

The rest of the nightmare was made more hideous still by the senseless racket of a dance band with the radio turned full volume. It was to keep her from hearing things, of course, though she didn't realize it at the time.

But she heard things anyway, in spite of the awful music, in spite of Mom's arms tight around her as they sat on the bed together, Mom's voice repeating over and over and over, 'Be still, honey, be still! Your daddy's taking care of everything.' She heard Pop's running steps again, then his voice as he bellowed up the stairway, to be heard above the radio. 'The key, Sally, the key! Where *is* it?'

Mom's voice, trying not to sound shaky and frightened. 'What key, Ben?'

'The *gun* cabinet. What in blazes do you think?' Never had Melanie heard him speak like that to Mom before, and never since.

More thudding footsteps then, more shrieking radio noise, and at last, in spite of everything, the thin, sharp, final-and-forever crack-crack-crack of Pop's deer rifle.

It was then that Melanie began to scream. She didn't want to scream, had no intention of doing so, and scarcely knew she was doing it. But somehow her mouth opened of its own accord and dreadful piercing sounds came out, again and endlessly again. Mom's face was only a blur in front of her, her words mere frantic noises. She had no idea of how much time went by before Pop loomed up above her bed and his hands reached towards her. His shirt was soaking wet and raindrops glistened among the curling blond hairs on his tanned forearms.

He lifted her to a sitting position and spoke to her, but his words seemed to have no meaning, and her screams went on. Then, in what seemed some kind of double explosion, he slapped her hard on both cheeks. Her last scream ended in a strangling sob and the whole house seemed to drop into a bottomless well of silence.

'There,' Pop said after a moment, sounding matter of fact but a little breathless. 'That's better.' He lifted her, stood her on her feet, and commanded, 'Take a lot of deep breaths. I'll be back in a second.'

He came back with a glass of water, which he handed her along with a little red capsule. 'All right now – chug-a-lug.'

Melanie couldn't say 'chug-a-lug' in response but did manage to swallow the pill.

'Sleeping pill,' Pop said. 'Nip into your pyjamas quick. You'll be sound asleep in five minutes.'

With a vast effort she fixed her eyes firmly on his belt buckle. 'Oh, Pop, I – ' Her throat closed down on the words and her eyes blurred.

'Pipe down!' Pop said sharply. He turned his back. 'Out of those clothes now, and into bed.'

When he leaned over to kiss her he said, 'We all make mistakes, bad ones. If we're smart, though, we learn from them all. You're smart, Mellie-girl.'

He straightened up and his voice seemed to come from far above her. Already her eyes were getting impossibly heavy. 'Now!' he said in a way that sounded decisive and final. 'That's the last I'm going to say. We won't talk about this. Not unless *you* want to – some time.'

It was nearly noon the next day when she struggled up from the depths of her drugged sleep. Her mind was a blank at first, then, bit by bit, recollection of the nightmare came. At first she thought it really had been a horrible dream from which she was now mercifully waking.

Before her foggy mind could focus on the truth, a sound got through to her ears, bringing her bolt upright in her bed. It came again, and this time there was no mistaking it. It was the high, thin, frightened squeal of a baby horse. In a flash Melanie was out of bed and in the middle of the floor, her dark hair wild around her face.

At that moment, Mom stepped into the room. Her smile was mysterious.

'What's . . .' began Melanie.

'Get into your jeans, quick,' Mom interrupted. 'And get down to the barn. Pop needs help.'

Melanie didn't know whether she put her clothes on upside down, backwards, or inside out, nor how she got down to the barn. She was only aware of having got there, breathless and a little dizzy.

She dashed through the barn, which was empty, and out into the corral, where she skidded to a halt, her eyes as round as a pair of harvest moons. The sight she saw would at any other time have sent her into whoops of laughter. Now she could only stare. In the middle of the corral stood Pop, the noon sun bright on his sweating face. He was carefully holding an empty pan as if he thought it were still full, though the oats lay scattered on the ground at his feet, and he was revolving slowly like a top about to run down. From his mouth came disjointed phrases, ridiculously plaintive, 'Whoa! Hey, whoa there, horsey, whoa! Take it easy, little guy!'

One quick glance was all Melanie could spare for Pop. Her eyes and every bit of her attention were seized and held by the racing figure of the most beautiful baby colt she had ever seen. Round and round the corral he went, his tiny hoofs beating a frenzied tattoo on the soft earth, his eyes showing white as they rolled in fear beneath his long, ridiculously girlish lashes. His silvery topknot that would some day be a forelock stood up in a way that seemed to express outrage as well as fright.

Vaguely she heard Pop's voice, '. . . strange place . . . first time away from his mother. . . .' He needn't have said anything at all. She knew what was going on in the colt's brain as well as if it had been her own. With no plan, merely doing what seemed natural, she watched the frantic little horse make yet another spin round the corral fence, then she stepped out away from the barn and stood directly in his path.

Catching sight of her, he flung up his head, eyes rolling more wildly than ever, stiffened his absurdly long forelegs, and slid to a halt not three feet away from her. His thin flanks heaved with the labour of breathing and his nostrils flared so wide she could see the pink skin inside.

Melanie and Orbit had met. They looked at each other – he with every nerve and muscle poised for instant flight if this new, strange human creature should prove dangerous, she with a look of rapturous wonder.

In a very low voice, without looking round, she said, 'Pop, you'd better go away. You're so big you scare him.'

'Hah!' said Pop, speaking jokingly but keeping his voice low. 'If I look big, you should see his mother!'

Properly ignoring this remark, Melanie kept her eyes on the colt, not moving. Pop began walking slowly, circling towards the barn door and keeping as far away from the motionless colt as possible. 'I know when I'm not wanted,' he said, trying to sound aggrieved but sounding relieved instead.

Melanie waited until his footsteps moved through the barn and died away on the other side. Then, slowly and carefully, making no sudden movement, she sank to a sitting position on the bare ground still damp from last night's rain, and began to talk.

Though he certainly didn't know it, the education of Orbit had begun.

He didn't know it any more than he knew, on that May afternoon four years later when he raised his nose from the grass, that it was twenty minutes after three. But he knew the sound the school bus made when it turned off the main highway and started up the Lark Hill road. He knew that soon it would appear from behind the grove of fir trees, pass along the front of it, and then, with an unpleasant screeching noise that made his ears twitch, come to a stop in front of the lane that led down from the house. Then the noisy smelly thing would clatter off, and there in its place would be Melanie.

On the bus, Melanie was busy watching a sight that presented itself every single schoolday except when the weather was too bad for Orbit to be out in the pasture. Every time it gave her the same lifting, soaring, bubbling thrill.

The bus nosed around the corner of the fir grove on the Hansen place, and there, in the far corner of the pasture, as far away from the road as he could possibly get, stood the great palomino stallion. His figure was as still as if he had been carved from rock, yet Melanie knew he was quivering all over.

At that instant the ageing bus roared and shook as Mr Penrose, who was both driver and janitor at Cascade, slammed into second gear and jammed his foot on the gas. 'Yippeeeee!' rang his familiar yell. 'This time I'm gonna win!' The bus staggered drunkenly forward, gaining a little speed.

That was the signal. At the far corner of the pasture the statue exploded into vivid life, and here came Orbit.

Breaking like a racehorse into a dead run, he aimed himself in an arrow-straight diagonal towards the corner of the pasture which the bus was approaching on its much shorter course.

The others on the bus saw this happen every day, just as Melanie did, but they couldn't help growing excited. They screamed and yelled encouragement to Mr Penrose, partly because it was natural for anybody to want to win a race, and partly because Mr Penrose never won except when it had been raining for days and the pasture was spongy beneath Orbit's churning hoofs.

14

The game was entirely Orbit's own idea. At first he had merely trotted along the fence at the roadside. But this was much too tame. The bus, even when it was two or three years younger, was no match for Orbit's high-stepping trot, and he would find himself fidgeting impatiently at the finishing point many seconds before the bus came to a stop. He had taken to letting the bus have a head start before racing it to the other side. That also was much too easy. The real race probably began by accident. Even Melanie didn't know, though she could see it in her mind, that at one time he had been lying asleep at the far corner and hadn't known the bus was coming until it passed the line of fir trees; then, at the last second, he raced for the goal. However it began, it had been the high point of his afternoon every schoolday since then. He never cheated, never gave himself a head start, not even when Mr Penrose cheated a little himself by shifting into second gear ahead of time to gain speed.

And now he came – ears flat to his tawny head, bright mane and tail rippling like the wake of a speeding boat. He was drawing closer, and Melanie could imagine she heard the drumfire of his hoofs along the solid path he had made for himself, the grunting intake of air into his tremendous lungs.

The yells inside the bus were deafening. Above them all rose Mr Penrose's falsetto 'Yippeeee!'

Melanie saw Orbit's running gait relax into a hand gallop, then to his easy, rocking canter, with his off foreleg in the lead, as it always was unless she signalled him to change. A few trotting steps, and there he was, standing in the corner as the bus creaked to a stop. There was an air about him of having been waiting patiently for hours.

'Smart Ellick ol' horse!' growled Mr Penrose as Melanie got off the bus. Melanie laughed as he slammed the doors behind her. He had been saying the same thing for about two years, but he always made it funny.

Books under her arm, she leaped the ditch beside the road with unconscious ease and let Orbit butt her head with his nose, his neck stretched over the fence. 'Smarty pants!' she said scornfully. 'You heard what the man said. Now simmer down; I've got a little work for you.'

He followed her with his eyes, ears, and nose as she hurried to the house to change. He gave a soft little snort. She was back again and the world was a very comfortable place to be in.

Chapter 2

MELANIE hurried into the house, with half her mind she was revelling in her freedom-at-last from the needlings of her classmates. With the other half she was probing uncomfortably into her own motives. What had made her write that insane thing on Conrad's questionnaire in the first place? Normal people didn't think about bringing horses into houses, did they? Much less tell the whole world about it.

This unprofitable train of thought was interrupted by a familiar sound coming from the kitchen.

It was one of Mom's alarm clocks, of course. Its little bell was ringing in the dragging, exhausted way that meant it had been ringing for a very long time. In the kitchen, using her ears like radar, she located the despairing clock in a cupboard just to the left of the refrigerator and shut off the alarm, feeling merciful.

The clock was one of a dozen – all large, cheap, ugly, and exactly alike – which Pop had given Mom as a birthday joke when Melanie was quite small. All twelve had been more or less constantly busy ever since.

This one was standing in the cupboard beside a frozen package with RUMP ROAST printed on it. The whole thing was as obvious as footprints in snow. Mom had got the roast out to defrost. It was defrosting in the cupboard so that Musclebound couldn't get at it. Musclebound was their huge black tomcat. The clock, of course, was to remind Mom it was time to put the roast in the oven.

Melanie closed the cupboard again, set the oven to preheat at 350 degrees, made herself a peanut-butter sandwich, and headed towards the attic to let Mom know what time of day it was.

To a stranger poking his head into the attic without advance warning, the sight of Mom at work would have been a start-ling experience. She sat silhouetted against the huge skylight Pop had built into the roof for her, with her legs twined like vines among the rungs of her high wooden stool, smeary pal-ette crooked in her left arm, brush in her right hand, head cocked at a belligerent angle as she eyed the half-finished painting on the easel.

The stranger would have had no clue to the fact that she was really a pretty woman, or, for that matter, that she was a woman at all. She was all but shapeless in an ancient T-shirt of Pop's with its sleeves cut off near the shoulders. Fore and aft it was streaked with every colour of paint known to art. Her hair, which fell, when permitted to, in soft heavy waves as black as outer space, was invisible now, turbanned in an old face towel for the purpose of keeping her paint-stained fin-gers out of it. On a stand beside her stool stood a paint box, a pickle jar from which blossomed a bouquet of long-handled brushes, a half-finished bottle of Coca Cola, and another alarm clock.

Melanie was swallowing her mouthful of sandwich in pre-paration for saying 'Hi' when the clock began to jangle des-pondently.

'Oh!' exclaimed Mom, looking wildly around as if she didn't know where the racket was coming from.

Melanie crossed to the stand and shut the little monster off. 'My goodness, are you home already?' she said.

Mom made a face at her. 'You *are* a witty one. Just like your father.' She stretched mightily, arching her back, then reached up and untwisted the towel, shaking the dark mass of her hair away from her face as it fell. 'How do you like it?' she asked, nodding towards the canvas. 'It's a completely new technique. I think I'm entering my neo-decadent phase.'

Melanie looked at the painting. 'Real colourful,' she said cheerfully, and added in a matter-of-fact tone, 'Alarm – roast – oven.'

'Ohgoodheavens!' Mom extricated her legs from the stool

and stood up – or rather down – and seized the bottom of the T-shirt with both hands. 'Hungry mouths, bottomless pits – ' she began, mimicking Melanie's tone. Whatever else she said was muffled in the T-shirt as she pulled it over her head.

About two minutes later, properly blue-jeaned and booted, Melanie started through the kitchen on her way to the barn. Mom, who was the very model of efficiency when she wasn't painting, was busy with the blender, making her special salad dressing. 'Will you set the table, dear?' she asked.

'It's Katie's turn,' Melanie said.

'She'll say it's Diane's.'

'Well,' Melanie said practically, 'she might be right at that.' She was going through the back door when Mom called, 'Your father's bringing a guest for dinner. Wear something civilized, will you, dear? And try not to smell too horsy.'

In the backyard between the two huge Norway spruces stood Katie's trampoline, on which she worked out violently on the random occasions when she remembered it was there, and on which Diane took her complex and scientific sunbaths amid a welter of bottles and vials of magical substances designed to aid the sun in turning female skin into a thing of unearthly beauty. At the moment it was occupied by Musclebound, looking huge, black, smug, and unemployed. Melanie gave a yank in passing at one of the trampoline's supporting ropes, just enough to jiggle him. He opened his eyes a slit, to prove he wasn't really asleep and that he didn't think she was being very funny. She felt a slightly wicked smile on her face at the thought of Diane's wounded cries when she discovered black hairs on her Searing Pink bathing-suit.

Rounding the tree and approaching the pasture fence, she found Orbit waiting as always, his neck stretched eagerly over the top rail, eyes and ears at attention. She reached up and rubbed him with her knuckles between the ears – as hard as she could, the way he liked it – and let him nibble her shoulder with his lips. Then she ducked and swung herself under the lower rail.

Orbit breathed moistly and happily down the back of her shirt.

She stood back, looking him in the eye. 'Okay,' she said. 'Time for you to go to work so you can keep your girlish figure. Want to go to work?'

He kept his eyes on her but didn't move.

'Hey!' she said sharply, 'I asked you a question. Want to go to *work*?'

He hesitated a moment, then shook his head violently. 'That's better,' Melanie said with satisfaction, adding, 'but you're going to anyway.'

It had taken her the better part of a month to teach him that trick. It was fun to amuse people with it, and to impress them with what appeared to be Orbit's ability to understand English. She knew that horses have very sensitive skins, particularly round their faces, and had discovered when Orbit was still a colt that he would shake his head in annoyance when she tickled him under the chin. Naturally, she had been careful from then on not to tickle him, but she didn't forget his reaction, and when the idea for the trick occurred to her the memory was still in her head, ready for use. After that it was merely a matter of patience. First she simply said 'Work?' in a questioning tone, then immediately tickled his chin and he shook his head to get rid of the tickle. Gradually the word itself became the same thing, in his mind, as the tickle; and after that he would shake his head at the sound of the word alone. It was fun for Melanie and no trouble for Orbit.

Her small hand under his jawbone, Melanie led him into the barn, past the entrance to his stall and into the tack-room Pop had built to her specifications. With the deftness of long practice, she bridled him, fastened the straps of her everyday saddle, and examined his feet for pebbles or clods, making him lift them one by one. He was barefoot now, but soon, with the winter rains over, the ground would get hard and he would need shoes. She led him outside, gathered the reins, and swung into the saddle. Nothing about Orbit moved except his ears, but she could feel his trembling eagerness to be off, to be moving.

She delayed giving him his signal, knowing that endless discipline was what it took to make any horse worth its salt. As for Orbit, he had no thought of anything so complicated as discipline. He merely knew that if he moved before he was told he would promptly be brought back and made to stand in exactly the same spot.

Melanie moved her left hand slightly, easing the pressure on the bit, and at the same instant pressed gently with her knees. Orbit's ears snapped forward and he moved off in his high-stepped, dainty walk, straight ahead, alert for the touch of a rein on his neck which would tell him which way to turn and when, or for a further slackening of the reins which would tell him he was free to step out into a trot. Melanie always kept him guessing, going clockwise round the pasture fence one time, counterclockwise another, or diagonally across to the far corner by the road. Today she took him round the pasture twice. Then they left the pasture and crossed a field into the lane that lay invitingly ahead, edged by gleaming trees.

Melanie let Orbit out little by little – from trot to canter to hand gallop – and then with her high, excited cry of 'Go, boy!' she leaned forward and laid her left hand with the knotted reins in it on the base of his neck just where his mane began. Orbit knew that he was free – free to move for the pure joy of it, free to flatten the arch of his neck and stretch his nose far forward so that the weight of his head was itself an aid in running, free to send the earth spinning behind him with the power of all his eight-hundred-odd pounds of bone and muscle and racing blood.

For Melanie, leaning forward with the whipping strands of his silvery mane just missing her face, the seat of her jeans barely touching the saddle, it was pure bliss. Her lips were parted in a smile that was half ecstasy and half astonishment. Her black ponytail with its scarlet ribbon streamed out behind her at exactly the angle of Orbit's tail. His strength was her strength, his speed her own, and the two of them shared an intelligence so blended and intermingled after four years of constant companionship that neither of them had any idea how much of it was hers and how much his. Certainly neither of them cared.

All too soon the fence at the lane's end loomed up ahead,

and with a shaky sigh Melanie lifted her hand from Orbit's withers and shifted her weight slightly back to let him know that it was time to stop flying and come back to earth.

The rest of the ride was more sedate, mainly because it was first uphill and then down. Going up, the trail was wooded and wild, following an old long-abandoned logging road. The far slope was less steep and the road wound along between small farms and nut orchards. The houses were either neat and modern or sprawling and old.

Melanie was kept busy replying to waves and friendly greetings from women working in their flower gardens, small children who rushed to the roadside with shrill questions and admiring looks. The looks were for Orbit, the questions for Melanie. She even broke one of her own rules, by permitting an overawed little four-year-old to feed him a dirty sugar lump, because the child's face, streaked by recent tears, could only be described as worshipful when he stared up at the majestic stallion.

Farther along, as they neared the Penfield place, Orbit's ears snapped forward and he tossed his head and gave his squealing bugle cry, in answer to a call she hadn't heard. Baldy of course. In a few moments they saw him: Ritchie Penfield's big chestnut gelding, straining his neck over the top fence rail.

There was no sign of Ritchie, though, and Melanie felt a momentary wave of disappointment, though she hadn't really expected he would be there. This was followed by another wave – of annoyance. She and Ritchie often rode together. He was a big, quiet boy, a year older than she, with none of the silly show-off ways of most of the boys she knew, and they talked as they rode – mostly about horses, but about all kinds of things, too. But he had a regrettable weakness that she completely failed to understand. When the first spring sunshine began to warm the land Ritchie promptly put on a baseball glove, and apparently he wore it from then until the end of summer. Not really, of course. Melanie had to admit in all fairness that Ritchie did a tremendous amount of work on the farm as well. He was a wizard with things mechanical, and all the machinery on the Penfield place was always in perfect working order. But he did spend every spare moment playing ball, so there was poor Baldy standing around getting fat through no fault of his own. It was a shocking waste of a good horse. Besides, Baldy was the only horse Orbit had ever met who didn't annoy him to the point of violence. Baldy was his friend.

Swallowing her annoyance, Melanie let Orbit leap the roadside ditch and smell noses with the big gelding. Baldy was no thing of beauty, with the comical splash of white that spread irregularly over his long face, but he was big and strong and filled with goodwill towards humankind. Melanie patted him affectionately and voiced her low opinion of his master before riding on.

After letting Orbit canter along the level last half mile, she pulled him up just above the boat-landing on the river, which had been her destination. It was one of her favourite spots. Until a few years ago when she was quite small it had been a ferry crossing. Now the paved ramp leading down to the water's edge was used for launching motor boats. On either side were mooring piers where people kept their boats during the spring and summer. There were three houseboats now, two of them new arrivals since the last time she had been there.

Melanie liked to sit on the bank and watch the colourful boats swooping up, down and across the river like noisy waterboatmen while Orbit rested and cooled down from his exercise. Orbit liked the place, too. It was shady and cool, and the grass grew lush and thick along the bank. She slid out of the saddle and let the reins fall, then loosened the saddle girth and hooked one stirrup over the saddlehorn. She didn't unsnap the bit from the bridle right away, testing him to see if the sugar lump episode had had any bad effect on his manners. It hadn't. He had known for too long that eating while bitted was bad manners to let one brief exception tempt him now. He permitted himself one wistful, sighing snort, to signify he knew perfectly well the grass was there and needing to be eaten, but he didn't lower his head. 'Good boy!' Melanie said, slapping his warm, moist neck; then she unsnapped the bit and dropped to a seat in the grass in front of him.

There were many things to watch: Mrs Ramsay, for one thing, dropping her baby in the river. This happened all the time, but it never stopped being funny. Mrs Ramsay was the young woman who lived in the first houseboat. The baby was brown as a nut and nearly as round. It had learned to walk but would much rather swim, and whenever it whooped whatever its word for 'swim' was, Mrs Ramsay picked it up, held it over the railing of the boat, and dropped it in. Melanie had never seen it without its little orange life-jacket, which covered all but its head and legs, and which was moored to the boat by six feet of heavy cord. Mrs Ramsay would then go back to her deck-chair and her book while the baby happily splashed until it was ready to be hauled in like a hooked fish.

Then there were the speed demons, who were dangers to themselves and to everyone else on the river. Today there were two of them – boys about Diane's age or older. Each had a little racing outboard, one red, one blue, and they were playing a game which apparently consisted of seeing how close they could come to killing each other without actually doing so. Starting in opposite directions, they would manoeuvre around, jockeying for position. Then they would open the throttles and zoom towards each other at top speed, the motors sounding like maddened hornets. At the last possible second they would sheer off, nearly swamping each other, and zoom away to start the suicidal game all over again.

Melanie was watching them with a kind of fascination, half hoping they wouldn't destroy each other and half hoping they would, when a stranger suddenly took a hand in the game.

Melanie saw the new boat long before the boys did. It appeared around the bend on the upper reach of the river, a long, low, black-and-silver launch heading for the landing at a moderate speed. It had reached a point perhaps three hundred yards from the landing when the little blue boat appeared, sweeping wide on a course that would take it straight across the stranger's bows. Melanie gasped and cried out. She could see that the boy at the little boat's wheel was looking back across his shoulder, intent on his opponent. He didn't even see the black-and-silver craft bearing down on him.

Violent collision seemed imminent when a powerful engine roared like a jet aircraft, and the black boat veered at almost a right-angle. Water creamed and boiled round the two boats, and the larger one shot away to the right, leaving the other jerking, bobbing, and swerving as the boy fought his wheel to keep afloat.

What happened next was pure joy to watch. Melanie had no more than let out, in a loud gasp, the breath she had been holding, when the blue boat, dangerously close to the river-bank, recovered itself and darted off to join its death-defying companion.

The rendezvous was never made. The black boat loosed its throaty roar again and came sliding relentlessly alongside the little one, overtaking it as easily as if it were powered by oars. Once alongside, the black one didn't sheer off but angled still closer until the bows were touching. Then, with remorseless efficiency, the big boat proceeded to nudge the little one straight into the river-bank, where it came to a halt with a visible jar.

Melanie, who found herself on her feet for a better view, felt so much like applauding that she was startled when she heard the sound of clapping hands. It was Mrs Ramsay. Catching Melanie's eye, she smiled brilliantly and clapped harder. 'Law and order comes to Tombstone!' she called.

A minute later the black boat slid neatly up to the dock and a tall man sprang out, painter in hand, made the boat fast, and stood looking around as if he expected somebody. Melanie stared at him, fascinated. He was almost as tall as Pop, though slimmer. He was dressed in dove-grey slacks, sneakers, and a sport shirt. She guessed he was about Pop's age, though his hair was streaked with grey. His face was exaggeratedly long and narrow, with deep-set dark eyes. An awfully homely man, Melanie was thinking. And then he smiled. It was like a happy ending to a scary story. There were lines of laughter every-where – around his eyes and mouth, in the humorous wrink-ling of his forehead, even in the funny cleft of his chin. Melanie found herself smiling, too. She couldn't help it.

And he wasn't even smiling at her. He was smiling at Mrs Ramsay, who had leaned over her rail and said in her reson-ant tone, 'Shiver my timbers, mate, why didn't you scuttle him?'

The stranger glanced upstream towards where the boy was

waist deep in the river, struggling to drag his boat free. 'I was tempted,' the man said, 'but my pirate's licence expired.' He paused, then said, 'You haven't seen a young fellow with a car, have you? California licence. He was supposed to – '

He stopped abruptly. Melanie, who was shamelessly eaves-dropping, felt her face grow hot. He had caught sight of her standing on the bank beyond the landing, her feet about on a level with his face. He stared so long and so intently that she was just starting to resent it when a sudden intuition made her feel silly. He wasn't looking at her. He was looking at Orbit.

His lips moved and she heard a long, low whistle that sounded almost like reverence. He crossed the landing and sprang to the bank beside her. Orbit raised his head from the grass, stopped chewing and shifted his feet uneasily. Melanie threw a quick look at his lips to see if the stranger had put him in a biting mood. But no teeth were showing. The man and the horse simply looked at each other. Then the man turned to Melanie with his startling smile and inclined his head in what looked like the beginning of a bow. 'My apolo-gies, Miss,' he said, 'for staring.' He glanced back at Orbit. 'Couldn't help it. He's that kind of horse.'

Ordinarily not inclined to judge people at first meeting, Melanie decided she liked this man very much indeed. It was the 'Miss' that did it. Most strangers his age called her 'little girl', which was awful, or 'young lady', which wasn't much better. She was trying to think of some clever way to return the compliment when he spoke again. 'Let me take a wild guess. His sire – could it be Astronaut?'

Melanie felt herself beginning to glow like a sunset. She nodded violently. 'Do you know Astronaut?'

'I rode him once.' He said it the way some men would say they had once shaken hands with the President. 'I even tried to buy him. But he wasn't for sale, not at any price.' He smiled again, this time a little sadly. 'I know it's a silly question, but – would you sell this one? And by the way, what do you call him?'

'Orbit,' Melanie said, then shook her head. 'No – no, I couldn't do that.' She literally could not imagine anything to buy with money – any amount of it – that she would rather have than Orbit. She added quickly, feeling sorry for the man. 'I'll let you ride him, though.'

His glance seemed a little startled. 'You would? How do you know I can handle him?'

Melanie shrugged. 'Same way you know he's worth buying.'

They stood smiling at each other like old friends who knew each other's thoughts.

'Mr Bristow, am I late, sir?'

They both jumped a little and turned. Melanie saw a tall, serious-looking young man standing at the fender of a low foreign car parked a little way up the ramp.

'Hello, Will,' the man named Bristow replied. 'No, you're not late. Find a motel?'

'Three miles down the highway, sir. Have a nice trip?'

'Perfect. Be with you in a second.' He turned back to Melanie. 'Sorry I can't take you up on your offer. I consider it an honour, though.' He stood looking at Orbit thoughtfully and Melanie had the flattered impression that he was reluctant to leave. 'Any idea what it takes to buy an Astronaut foal these days?'

A little chagrined at her ignorance on so important a subject, Melanie had to admit that she didn't.

'I'm a nosy old man,' he said apologetically. 'But tell me – did your father give him to you?'

Melanie nodded.

In an oddly wistful way he said, 'He must love you very much.' He thrust out his hand, shook hers as briskly as he might the hand of another man, and then was gone, leaving Melanie a little breathless.

Mrs Ramsay's voice interrupted her thoughts. 'Looks like you've found a new admirer.'

'Not me,' Melanie said. 'Orbit.'

'Well, come on down and have some fresh-baked cookies. They look more like potato chips, but they're good.'

Melanie did, and they were. She stood on the dock chatting easily with Mrs Ramsay, who always managed to act as if there were no difference in their ages. Speculating on the stranger's identity, Mrs Ramsay said, 'I'll bet he's a temporarily unemployed ambassador waiting for a new country to start up.'

'Well, he's certainly somebody important,' Melanie agreed. 'And he knows about horses.'

Mrs Ramsay looked down at her, laughing. 'And that, of course, makes him even more important than an ambassador. Well, nothing would surprise me, the way the great world is moving in on our little oasis here. Did you notice I've got new neighbours?' She nodded towards the other two houseboats. 'The people in the first one there are an older couple. He's a retired Navy man.'

The boat, Melanie saw, was freshly painted in gay colours and looked as neat as a well-kept tack-room.

'I don't know who lives on the other one,' Mrs Ramsay went on, 'but if they're as shabby as their boat I don't want to know them.'

The third houseboat, moored at the far end of the dock, apparently as far away from the others as it could get, was large and ungainly. It looked rather like a floating barn that hadn't known the touch of a paint-brush for about twenty years. Through its partly open door Melanie could see into its gloomy interior and she glimpsed the figure of a man sprawled in a chair, wearing a torn vest. He struck a match as she looked and held it to his pipe, wreathing in smoke an indistinct face that seemed to need a shave as much as the boat needed paint.

Mrs Ramsay made a small snorting sound. 'It's a cinch *he's* no ambassador. Well, come on in and entertain me while I get dinner.'

'Oh gee, dinner!' Melanie said, suddenly reminded of the time.

'Have dinner with us – we'd love it!' Mrs Ramsay glanced over Melanie's shoulder towards Orbit with a quick smile. 'And bring Pegasus. I'm sure he has lovely table manners.'

Melanie looked at her rather sharply but decided quickly that Mrs Ramsay couldn't be teasing her. There was no way in the world she could have heard about Conrad's newsletter. The thought made her stumble a little over her words as she declined the invitation.

Mrs Ramsay didn't notice, though. 'Well, next time then,' she said. 'I can always throw an extra onion in the stew.'

Chapter 3

ON the ride home Orbit found himself free – within limits – to choose his own gaits. Only part of Melanie's mind was on him. The rest was taken up with thoughts of the strange Mr Bristow. He was obviously rich – or anyway very well-off. The boat, the car, the man who called him 'Sir' – all of them proved that.

And the thing he had said about Pop. 'He must love you very much.' Well, of course he did. Melanie had no doubt about that. But what Mr Bristow obviously meant was that Pop must have paid an awful lot of money for Orbit. And Pop wasn't rich. He could have been, maybe, but he wasn't.

Mom had explained it one time. 'Your father's an artist, honey. He'd just laugh if you called him that, but it's true – and artists don't often make a lot of money. He could be a contractor – just do the figuring and the planning and the over-seeing. That way he could have a lot of jobs going at the same time, with other men doing the work. That's the way they make money in the building business. He even tried it for a while and was doing well, but he was miserable.'

'Why?' Melanie demanded, unable to see how anybody could be miserable while making a lot of money.

'Because he just can't keep his hands off the tools,' Mom said. 'Any more than I can keep mine off these silly paint brushes. He's got to *feel* a house grow, not just see it. He carries in his mind a sort of vision of the perfect house – the kind that would make a person glad just to be in it, the kind that doesn't have a single door that sticks, and there aren't any draughts in wintertime and all the lights are in just the right places, and everything about it is beautiful. He's never built that perfect house, and he never will, but he has the *vision*, and that's the important thing, Mellie. So he does the planning and all the rest of it, but he works for wages. They're very good wages, of course, but they'll never make us rich.'

So there it was. Pop wasn't rich, and yet he had gone out that awful night Melanie dared not think about, and managed to buy for her the finest colt that could be found. Until now she had never given a thought to how much it cost, to how many hours of Pop's work the price of Orbit represented. It must have been a lot of hours and days and weeks, if what Mr Bristow was hinting at was right. And she had never given it a thought.

From the beginning, of course, she had known *why* he did it, though neither of them ever spoke of it. He had wanted to give her, instantly, a new animal to love, one that would keep her constantly busy and drive from her mind the horror of Gigi's death. But more than that, he had wanted to show her he had faith in her, that he knew she would never again let an animal come to harm through her carelessness, that he would trust her with the finest horse that money could buy.

She was so lost in her thoughts that she paid no attention to her surroundings and was suddenly awakened to the fact that she was back in the orchard again. What woke her was that Orbit, feeling her hand slack on the reins, decided it was a wonderful time to cover a lot of ground in a hurry. He broke from a trot to a gallop with a lunge that would have toppled a less knowing rider. Melanie's slim but wiry body did all the right things without her brain having to trouble itself at all, and before Orbit had really got into his stride he found himself pulled sharply to a walk and pointed towards home.

In the tack-room she was starting to unsaddle when she heard Orbit make a soft, delicate little snorting noise. She paused momentarily, sniffing the air, then smiled a little slyly and said in tones loud enough to be heard in the hayloft, 'Orbit, we've got company.'

There was a rustling sound above and in a moment Katie's head and shoulders were framed in the square opening at the top of the stationary ladder that gave access to the loft. Her face was wearing what Pop called her 'friendly fiend' expression, accentuated by the soft halo of her hair which looked even more angelically golden than usual against the darkness of the loft. (The gold was a rinse, but Melanie thought it looked lovely all the same.)

'You little stinker!' exploded the friendly fiend. 'How do you always *know*? I didn't make a sound. I didn't even *exhale*! Aren't you ever going to *tell* me?'

'I've already told you,' Melanie said, dragging the heavy saddle from Orbit's back and heaving it on to its barrel-shaped wooden support. 'It's like radar or something – I just *know*.' She had been enjoying this mysterious power for a long time and couldn't bear to give away its secret.

It was really quite simple. She and Orbit could smell Katie, who took at least one bath a day and sometimes as many as three. Her bath-taking was scornfully referred to by Diane as her 'hobby', which wasn't quite fair, because her real hobby was reading books. The baths, of course, didn't interfere with her reading. She dumped bubble powder into the tub, let the water run until the foam piled high above the top of the tub, then climbed in and disappeared, all but head, hands, and book. The result was that she went around exuding soapy fragrances. These weren't particularly noticeable in most places but in the barn with its odours of horse, hay, leather and saddlesoap, they left a trail that Orbit and Melanie couldn't help picking up instantly, like a pair of bloodhounds.

'Oh, all right, have your childish little secrets,' Katie said good-naturedly. Her head disappeared from the opening to the loft and in a moment her legs appeared as she started down the ladder. She was wearing shorts and Melanie had her usual twinge of regret that Katie had to have such big legs. They were a nice shape, but big. Poor Katie had to be the one to inherit Pop's size – or anyway some of it. She had inherited his blondness, too, which was a help, and his disposition, which made everybody love her, but she somehow just missed being pretty. It wasn't fair, Melanie often thought, to be big and not quite pretty, with a sister like Diane around. Maybe Katie didn't care, though, because she was so clever. She was always reading books about things that even Mom and Pop knew nothing about, and when she wasn't reading she was writing something.

She sat down on a bale of hay and watched while Melanie got the brush and comb and went to work on Orbit. That is, she seemed to be watching; Melanie could tell that her mind, as usual, was busy in ways that had nothing to do with what was in front of her eyes.

Katie straightened abruptly and said, 'Oh, I knew there was something I was supposed to tell you.'

'Dress up for dinner,' Melanie said promptly. 'And don't smell too horsy.'

'Right. Mom *is* a dreamer, isn't she. Oh, yes – and be ready for dinner at seven.'

When Katie had gone Melanie paused in her chore and looked thoughtfully at the door through which she had disappeared. The door, opening into the lane between two huge lilac bushes, was an ordinary people-sized door, not designed for horses. The same size as the front door of the house. She looked from the door to Orbit, comparing their sizes. Orbit looked amazingly big. Then she slipped a halter over his head, snapped a lead rope into it, and led him to the little door. 'We're going to do something new and different,' she told him, unconsciously raising her voice to the pitch that had been

34

natural to it when she and he were four years younger – the tone she knew he liked best to listen to. 'And who knows how handy it might be some day if you learn how to duck.'

Half an hour later she brought the lesson to an abrupt close. She was sweaty and tired and Orbit was starting to get stubborn. There was that wild sort of look in his eyes that told her he had reached the limits of his patience and ability to concentrate.

After a false start or two and a lot of sweet talk, he had ducked his head and gone through the door, but he had done it in a leaping lunge and Melanie had to make him do it over and over until he could be mannerly about it. Then she had started getting him to back through it. That was when he began to look wild, and to his relief she took him into his stall, filled his oat box, threw a slab of hay into his manger and hurried to the house.

The kitchen was steamy and filled with meaty fragrances. Melanie realized she was ravenous as well as weary. As she started up the back stairs, Mom called warningly, 'Fifteen minutes, Mellie – and *do* look nice!'

'O-*kay!*' she flung back. She was tired of being reminded to look nice. As if she always went around looking like a wet dog or something.

In her room she kicked off her boots and dashed for the bathroom, unbuttoning her shirt as she went. At the bathroom door she skidded to a halt and said, 'Gad!'

Diane, a flawless dream in white, was in front of the mirror examining the back of her sleek head with the aid of a hand mirror. She gave Melanie a glance and wrinkled her nose. '*Really,* Melanie,' she said. 'You smell like a – a livestock pavilion!'

'Gad!' said Melanie again, 'what are you being queen of tonight – the Webb family?'

'Father,' Diane began in her most infuriating manner, 'has a *guest* for dinner.' Calling Pop 'Father' was a recent development with Diane. 'A very distinguished guest,' she added. 'I hope you'll try not to disgrace us.'

'I won't spit on the floor, if that's what you mean.' Melanie yanked off her shirt and dropped it on the floor.

She remembered she had made a good resolution to be nice to her sister. But this just didn't seem to be the time for it. Unbuttoning her jeans and shucking them off, she said, 'I've only got ten minutes, and you've probably been in here for two hours, so' – she reached into the shower stall and flipped the handle – 'so watch out or you'll get *splashed*!'

About twelve minutes later, smelling a little more like Katie than like Orbit, and looking, she thought, as presentable as the occasion demanded, she sailed down the front stairs, rounded the corner of the hall, headed into the living-room with a full head of steam, and all but ran straight into the arms of Mr Bristow, who was just getting up from the chair next to Pop's.

His eyebrows shot up at a comical angle as he straightened to his full height. Then his smile appeared. 'This is too nice to be true,' he said.

Melanie started to open her mouth to say something and found it was already open.

'My daughter Melanie,' said Pop.

'Come to dinner, everybody,' said Mom.

Chapter 4

I<small>T</small> didn't occur to Melanie until weeks later to wonder if Mr Bristow actually got anything to eat that evening. Her memory could see numerous pictures of his fork starting up to his mouth with a cargo of food. There were a lot of other pictures of the fork pausing half-way up and then going slowly back down to his plate while he politely answered one of the questions hurled at him.

Whether he left the table hungry or not, he certainly left it without any secrets from the Webb girls – except, of course, the secrets that were important to him.

His first name was Luke – shortened, understandably, from Lucretius. 'My father,' he explained, 'wanted me to be a great philosopher.' Instead, he had become a producer of television shows. He lived in Beverly Hills, worked in Hollywood, travelled all over the world, and knew so many of what Diane called 'really important' people that she was 'speechless'.

Until he was twelve years old he had lived on a farm not ten miles from where the Webbs lived now, and in spite of all his travels he had never been able to get Oregon out of his mind. Three months ago he had bought a place as much like the place of his boyhood as he could find, had inquired around

37

as to who was the finest builder of houses in the area, and here he was. After dinner he and Pop would disappear into Pop's study and talk house. Pop was excited about it. Melanie could tell that the 'vision' Mom talked about was working inside him. Maybe this would be his chance to build the perfect house.

Mr Bristow turned to Melanie as they were all getting up from the table at last and said, 'I've been thinking about that horse of yours. May I see him again before I go?'

'You can see him now,' Melanie said promptly.

'Later, Mellie,' Pop said. 'Just now Mr Bristow wants to tell me about his house plans.'

It was Melanie's turn to help with the dishes. She was at the sink, scraping the plates while Mom finished clearing the table, when there was a sudden roar of men's voices from the study. Melanie nearly dropped a plate. Surely they couldn't be fighting! Then Mom came in with her hands full of dishes and her face full of amusement. 'Keep your ears covered, Mellie,' she said. 'They've just discovered they were both with the First Marines in the South Pacific. Mr Bristow isn't Mr Bristow any more; he's 'Old Brass Bottom'. Your father is something known as "Cuddles Webb, the nightmare of BHQ", whatever that may be.' She laughed as she put her load down. 'There goes the house planning. They'll be in there half the night fighting the war.'

'No, they won't,' Melanie said, forgetting that flat contradictions were impolite. 'Mr Bristow's going to come out and see Orbit.'

'I wouldn't count on it, honey,' Mom warned.

The war and Pop's part in it never seemed quite real to Melanie, who wasn't born until it was all over.

Finishing her chore with her customary quick efficiency she went up to her room, where she slipped out of her skirt and eyed the jeans she had left on the floor. It didn't seem right to wear those dirty old things while she showed Orbit, even just to an audience of one.

She got out her jodhpurs and a clean white shirt and put

them on, enjoying as she always did the tight clasp of the jodhpurs around her legs. Her dress boots could have done with a little polishing, but she put them on anyway.

In the barn she heard Orbit's softly nickered greeting from the corral. Taking the canvas off her English saddle, she shook the dust and bird droppings off it. It was a nuisance to have to keep everything covered, but she couldn't bear to let Pop get rid of the swallows' nest up under the roof. She missed their spritely twittering when they were gone for the winter, and had a notion Orbit missed it, too.

The saddle looked all right, but she got a clean cloth and polished it anyway. While she was doing it she heard the thud of hoofs outside, then inside, and could feel Orbit's eyes on her as he stood peering across his manger into the tack-room. When he made his delicate little snorting sound, she smiled. 'Okay, so I took a bath! Do you mind?'

If he did mind he didn't say anything about it. Melanie put the cloth away and looked at him for the first time. 'Hah! So you had to go and roll!' There were streaks of dust along his back and barrel. She was getting a brush out of the cabinet when he whirled and disappeared at a trot into the darkness of the corral, where he loosed a sharp call into the night. Instantly it was answered from the back end of the pasture.

Baldy. Which of course meant Ritchie. An unreasoning annoyance took hold of Melanie. Why, when he hadn't even been around for almost a week, did he have to show up now? Now, when Mr Bristow might come out just any minute? She started polishing the saddle again, needlessly. When Ritchie came slouching through the corral door she was further annoyed to see he was wearing his baseball shirt along with his jeans. Riding a horse in a baseball shirt – how silly could he get?

'Hi, Mellie,' Ritchie said in the boyish voice that hadn't made up its mind to change completely, even though he was the biggest boy in the freshman class at high school. That annoyed her, too.

'Well,' she said acidly. 'You mean the New York Giants can spare you for a while?'

'New York Mets,' Ritchie said. 'The Giants are in San Francisco. What's wrong?'

'Nothing's wrong. Did you bring a baseball? We could play catch or something.'

He looked at her oddly but merely said, 'Thought we might ride somewhere. Say, you're all dressed up. Something going on?'

'I'm not "all dressed up". I'm simply *clean*. And there's nothing going on. We simply happen to have a guest tonight, a very important man. And in about five minutes he's coming out here and – '

Melanie broke off, her words echoing inside her head. Gad! she said to herself. I sound just like Diane!

'I get it,' Ritchie said, hoisting himself by his hands to a precarious seat on the edge of the manger. 'You don't want some local yokel standing around gawking while – '

'Oh Ritchie, I didn't mean that. I only – '

'I know just how you feel. If I had somebody important coming – you know, like a scout from the big leagues or something – I wouldn't want *you* to come barging in and – '

He stopped so abruptly that Melanie halted her pointless polishing and glanced up at him. There was a puzzled frown on his broad, good-natured face. 'That's funny,' he said, apparently talking more to himself than to her.

'What's funny?'

'I–I guess I *wouldn't* really mind.' He added quickly, 'I really just came over to tell you about something that happened this evening. Something sort of peculiar.'

Melanie got out a brush. 'Well, come on and tell me while I clean Orbit up a little.'

Ritchie scrambled out of the manger and followed her out to where Orbit and Baldy were communing in comradely silence. 'Fellow stopped by just before dinner,' he said. 'Wanted to know if I'd sell Baldy. There was something funny about him.'

'What do you mean, funny?'

'Well, for one thing, he said he was from California, but I saw he had a Nevada licence. Besides, I – well, I just didn't like him. He gave me that old buddy-buddy bit. You know, like we were the same age.'

'Well, how old was he?' Melanie asked, wondering why all this mattered enough to bring Ritchie all the way over to tell her about it.

'Oh, twenty-five or so. He called me "pardner"!'

'Oh, ughhh!' Melanie said, and Ritchie went on. 'He really didn't want to buy Baldy at all. He was trying to pump me, so I played dumb and let him talk. He said his job was buying horses for a string of riding stables down in California, and that he'd heard there were some good ones around this area. He said these stables were real fancy ones and didn't use anything but palominos.'

'Then what did he want with Baldy?'

'That's what I mean,' Ritchie said. 'But he thought I wouldn't notice the slip – me being the village idiot, standing there with my mouth open and saying "Gee, mister", every once in a while. Anyway, he talked on and on and finally mentioned he'd heard something about a palomino stallion around here and – '

Melanie pounced on that one too. 'Stallion! They don't almost *never* use stallions in riding stables!'

'Of course not! So that's how I know the guy's a phony.' He hurried on. 'This'll sound sort of crazy, but I figured he's nosing around trying to locate Orbit.'

'Orbit!' said Melanie so loudly that Orbit swung his head around to stare at her. 'But Ritchie, that's silly! Why should he want to nose around? Anybody can tell him where I live. Then all he has to do is knock on the door and say, "I'll give you a million dollars for your horse," and I'll say, "No thanks," and he'll go away and that's all there is to it.'

Ritchie started to say something else, but apparently changed his mind. 'Guess you're right,' he said, sounding unsatisfied. 'Well, I'd better get home. Practice session before school in the morning.' He vaulted over the fence and picked up Baldy's reins.

Melanie felt a return of her earlier annoyance – not with Ritchie especially, just with baseball. It had always struck her as such a stuffy sort of game, with everybody doing the same silly things over and over again.

'Well,' she told Ritchie, 'when you go to bed be sure to wrap up the old pitching arm in cotton wool.'

'I don't pitch,' Ritchie said loftily, 'I catch.' He swung himself aboard Baldy.

'Okay,' Melanie said, 'then go wrap up the old *catching* arms.'

He grinned as he wheeled the reluctant Baldy away and trotted off into the darkness. The last thing Melanie saw by the weak light from the stable door was the big red '12' on the back of his shirt.

Orbit raised his head and shrieked a heart-rending farewell into the night.

By the time fifteen minutes had passed Melanie wished she had urged Ritchie to stay awhile. A person could talk to a horse just so long – even a horse like Orbit – and then it became a matter of merely talking to one's self, which wasn't very rewarding.

She put in some of the time giving Orbit practice in being led around blindfolded. This was the first step on a long-range plan. It might take years, but eventually she hoped to ride him in a special show event with the blindfold on, putting him through all his gaits, doing everything he would normally do, except of course jumping. She had seen this done two years before, at the big show at Pendleton, and had never forgotten it.

Orbit was a long way from being able to give her that quality of trust. The blindfold was too new to him, and too frightening. Besides, it was probably uncomfortable. She had designed it herself, and Diane had cut and sewed it for her.

Diane, surprisingly, was very good at sewing and liked to do it. The trouble, Melanie had decided, was that the blindfold needed some sort of arrangement that would hold the cloth away from Orbit's eyelashes. It would need a lot of thinking about.

After leading him in and out of the barn a few times, and once around the corral, she took the blindfold off and sat down to study it on the bunk bed Pop had built for her in the tack-room. Gradually she became aware that there was a late feeling around her. No cars were going by on the road and there was a chill to the air that hadn't been there before. She looked at the clock – one of Mom's big ugly ones – but as usual she had forgotten to wind it. She tossed the blindfold aside impatiently and went out to the corral, startling Orbit, who was standing, probably asleep, with the weight of his hindquarters on one foot. The moon had come up, along with an impetuous little breeze, and together they turned the hairs of his mane and tail into tiny streamers of incandescent fog. He swung his head to look at her.

In spite of the fact that her mind was occupied at the moment with other things, she couldn't help pausing long enough to let the picture of him print itself on her mind. Then she said, softly but sharply, 'Ho, boy!' to warn him she was coming, took three running steps, grabbed a handful of mane, and vaulted to his back. Using another handful of mane to guide him, she rode along the pasture fence towards the front of the house. She had to satisfy herself that Mr Bristow was still there.

Orbit ambled along willingly enough but at a sort of plough-horse walk because he was sleepy and because, after all, she wasn't asking him to do anything a plough-horse couldn't have done just as well.

They were just coming abreast of the front part of the house, from which lights streamed out across the lawn, when Orbit suddenly stopped. At the same instant his head jerked up and his ears twitched forward. 'Hey!' said Melanie a little

43

crossly, 'I didn't say stop!' She squeezed with her knees and he started forward again, wide awake now. She could feel a new alertness in the springiness of his stride, and he turned his head once to peer towards the shadowy far corner of the pasture.

Melanie halted him at a point opposite the window of Pop's study. The room was still lighted, and though from that angle she couldn't see inside she could hear the low rumble of voices. The foreign car still stood in the driveway beyond. She sighed with exasperation, wondering if Mom was right after all and the men really were going to talk all night. She pulled Orbit's mane towards the left, and as he turned she was startled into alertness by the sound of a car motor starting. It came from a point across the road from the far side of the pasture, where the Carlsons' fir grove cast a velvety shadow over everything. Orbit had already seen, smelled, or heard something or somebody there. She stared towards the spot, expecting to see the car's lights come on. But they didn't and she could tell by the sound of the motor that the driver was easing away in the darkness as noiselessly as possible.

A chill ran up her back, but then she remembered about the stupid high school boys who sometimes came skulking around hoping for a glimpse of Diane, or perhaps checking up on who might be coming to see her.

Back in the tack-room again, she found herself staring at the blank, uninformative face of the clock. She snatched it down from the shelf, wound it and set it by guess. It began ticking clankily away, telling time like mad without, as far as Melanie could tell, ever moving its hands. Plunking herself down on the bed because there wasn't anything else to do, she eyed the softly gleaming saddle and felt a little forlorn and just a shade resentful. Since it was as easy to feel resentful lying down as sitting up, she flopped down, folding her arms under her head, and stared up at the rafters high above. In their nest the swallows chittered petulantly, as though they were saying, 'For heaven's sake, turn off the light so we can get some sleep.'

Ten or fifteen minutes later Orbit ambled in, his hoofs thudding softly on the layer of straw and shavings that carpeted his stall. He lowered his head and sniffed delicately, then raised it and looked across the manger to the tack-room where Melanie lay. She didn't move. A cool breeze rippled deliciously along his back and ruffled his mane. He watched her hopefully, his ears pointed sharply forward, but after a while he swung around and ambled out again to smell the interesting night smells and to see if any tufts of grass had grown in the bare corral since the last time he had looked.

For Melanie the dream never came quietly the way good dreams came. It came like an evil wind, from some formless cruel wasteland, where even the trees and the rocks and the endless sand were full of fear and foreboding. And she could never stop it, never head it off, though part of her seemed always to be fighting to keep it from coming nearer. It didn't come as frequently now as it had in the years past, but when it did it was always the same in effect, though the details varied, and it was always horrible beyond imagining.

Sometimes Orbit was there – not the great, powerful Orbit of now, but the baby Orbit of then, with his little topknot bristling and his huge eyes full of fear. But usually it was Gigi. While Melanie watched from somewhere far below, the little mare stood high on a ledge of rock overlooking a vast expanse that might have been the sea but might also have been a boundless swamp with vapours rising from it. The wind was always blowing towards her, flattening her mane along her back, while behind her, creeping ever closer through the dense shadow of trees that writhed in the wind, was a Thing of incredible menace. The Thing took many forms, none of them like anything that ever existed in the real world.

Whatever form it took, Gigi never saw it. But Melanie saw it. She ran screaming to warn Gigi. The path was littered with the twisted branches of fallen and rotting trees. Brambles tore at her legs, stones tripped her, she fell, struggled up, fell again, never getting any farther, and all the time the

45

Thing was coming closer. Still Gigi did not hear. Melanie had to make her hear – *had* to – and she screamed louder, louder, *louder* into the teeth of the roaring wind. Gigi – *Gigi* – GIGI! ... The world did a sickening swoop, the sound of her own gasping breath was loud in her ears, her wildly struggling body was held tight, Pop's rough cheek was pressed against her own, the smell of his clothes and shaving lotion swirled around her like a heavenly perfume, and his voice repeated again and again, 'It's all over, Mellie-girl, all over.'

Melanie shamefully put off the moment of opening her eyes and letting Pop know she was awake. Finding herself wrapped in his comforting strength filled her with a sense of bliss so all-encompassing that she couldn't keep herself from making it last just a little longer than it needed to. Thinking about it later, she always felt sheepish and cross with herself. She was fourteen, much too old to be cradled and comforted like a baby.

Pop, who seemed almost to read her mind, must have known how she felt, because the moment she stopped struggling he quickly put her on her feet, though he kept one arm around her shoulders.

Her knees felt shaky and her voice was tremulous. 'Oh, Pop, did I make an awful racket?'

'Deafening,' Pop said, smiling. 'I was just – '

'OH!' Melanie clapped her hands to her lips, eyes wide above them. 'Did Mr Bristow hear me?'

'He's gone, honey. Which reminds me: this may all be my fault. He told me twice he'd asked you to show Orbit for him, and I kept putting him off. I was too wrapped up in his house plans. If I'd let him come, you wouldn't have gone to sleep and – ' He shrugged regretfully.

'That's silly,' she told him firmly, happy for the chance to reassure *him* for a change. 'How can it be your fault that I have a dream?'

They crossed to the door. Pop switched off the light and

they started towards the house. Once Melanie paused. 'Pop, do you think I'll ever stop? The dreams, I mean?'

Pop hesitated a long time. Then he said, 'To be honest, I just don't know. We'll hope they stop as you get older. But the human mind is a strange and wonderful thing – a little frightening when you think about it. It never forgets – way down underneath, I mean. This may be a thing you'll have to live with. We all have things like that, buried down deep. But we can handle them – and if we can, we've got to.'

They walked on. The moon was high now and bright enough to make grey shadows around their feet. Pop took her hand again and she felt oddly shy. 'Do you have things like that?' she asked.

'Lots of them.'

'What kind of things?'

She felt his hand tighten. 'The war,' he said. Then he laughed softly. 'We're a serious pair, aren't we? Now let's both fall into bed without even looking at a clock.'

At the door to her room he put his hand on her head and roughed her hair a little. Suddenly she felt very tired, but very calm and relieved and free, as though something funny had happened instead of something dreadful.

'Pop,' she said, 'did they *really* call you "Cuddles"?'

He kissed her and gave her a sharp spank at the same time. 'I'll deny it with my dying breath. 'Night, honey.'

When she opened her window before getting into bed, Melanie glanced sleepily out into the moonlit pasture and remembered the car Diane's secret admirer had driven stealthily away. She should have mentioned it to Pop, who didn't like that sort of thing. She was making up her mind to do so when she fell into a blessedly dreamless sleep.

Chapter 5

MELANIE didn't get a chance to mention anything to Pop in the morning. By the time she had dressed and gone down to the kitchen where Mom was bustling around, he had already gone to work.

'He plans to work early and late to finish the job he's on,' Mom explained, 'so he can get started by the first of July on Mr Bristow's.' She laughed. 'He can hardly wait. Mr Bristow told him to build it just as he would his own house. The best of everything and hang the expense. Pop's like a boy turned loose in a candy store.'

'Will he – Mr Bristow – be coming back?' Melanie asked.

'He'll have to. Pop's already making lists of things they didn't get around to talking about last night. Hey! You come back here and eat something decent!'

Melanie had snatched up a doughnut in passing and headed for the back door. 'Ten minutes to bus time,' she replied, a bite already in her mouth. She went out before Mom had a chance to say anything else.

In the stable Orbit greeted her with his usual impatient breakfast-time nicker. 'Okay, *okay*,' she told him. 'Just hold your people!' Reaching under the manger's overhang, she detached two slabs of hay from the bale there and put them in the manger. She stuffed more doughnut into her mouth and watched with satisfaction as he started to eat. Then she stepped outside the corral door to make sure the automatic mechanism that kept his water-tub full was working properly. When he was younger he had occasionally amused himself by mashing with his teeth the little copper float that controlled the flow of water. The result, on one occasion, had been that the water ran all night long, making a swamp of the corral and running the well dry so that there wasn't a drop of water in the house for about five hours.

Returning to the tack-room, she interrupted Orbit long enough to rub noses, and hurried back to the house.

Mom, who had seen her coming, was standing determinedly in the middle of the kitchen, holding a glass of milk. This she thrust at Melanie, and stood watching to make sure she drank it all. 'Sometimes,' she said, 'I'm tempted to bring that horse right in here and plunk him down at the breakfast table. Maybe *then* you'd eat a proper breakfast.'

Melanie stopped gulping her milk for a moment and stared wide-eyed at Mom over the rim of the glass. Was Mom an unconscious mind reader or something?

Katie, who was at the table energetically disposing of a large bowl of cereal, made a hooting sound. 'Don't worry about Mellie, Mom. She eats oats in the barn. Buckets of them – lovely, crunchy, vitamin-packed – '

'Kate-eeeeeeeee!' Diane's feet pounded down the stairs and she burst indignantly into the kitchen. 'Katie, have you been using my *Arpège*?'

Katie deliberately took another mouthful of cereal and talked through it. 'Don't be silly. I prefer my own lovely, natural fragrance, unimpaired by – '

'Then who left the stopper out of the bottle?'

'Mellie did. She uses it on Orbit. *Drenches* him with it. He smells nicer than any horse I ever – '

'Oh Katie, do hush up!' Mom interposed. 'Diane, you probably left the stopper out yourself. Now eat something quick, before – '

Melanie set her glass down with a clatter. 'Hey-there's-my-bus-g'bye!' She dashed out through the living-room, scooping up en route the books she had brought home and never looked at, slammed the front door behind her and flashed down the drive and across the road just as Mr Penrose's bus came squealing to a halt.

At the school, to her great relief, she found that everybody seemed to have abandoned Melanie Webb in favour of other topics of conversation. Everybody but Conrad Wemmer, who waylaid her after lunch. Wearing his odious knowing look and of course his ears, which stood out from his narrow head like jug handles, he came straight to the insufferable point. 'Well, I suppose you've got that horse wearing bedroom slippers by this time!'

Suppressing a crushing rejoinder which wouldn't have got anywhere anyway with the uncrushable Conrad, Melanie said, a bit loftily, 'I'm really very *tired* of the subject, Conrad. What do you say we drop it?'

She should have known better. Conrad all but crowed like a rooster. 'I thought so!' he exulted. 'You never even meant to do it. You only *said* you would!'

Melanie strove mightily with her temper, which was not an explosive one. Since she had to express herself somehow, she tried the haughty routine with which Diane had made her all too familiar. 'You have such a *juvenile* mind, Conrad,' she informed him. 'I suppose you'll just have to see with your own beady little eyes. Very well, you'll be hearing from me.' With that she stalked off down the hall.

Whatever satisfaction she got out of the toplofty speech evaporated by the time she had taken a dozen steps, and in no time at all she was calling herself names for having let

Conrad Wemmer goad her a second time into words she bitterly regretted. She spent the rest of the schoolday in a state of depression.

What made the whole thing ghastly was that she had made public property of what was, and should have remained, a private project. Actually, it hadn't been a project at all but merely a sort of yearning – and no doubt foolish – aspiration. Now it had become something she had to do for the sake of her stubborn pride, and the joy was gone from it.

She had no idea when the thought of bringing Orbit into the house had first occurred to her, or why, but it had been around a long time, and every now and then she got it out and played with it, like a miser with a piece of gold, then stowed it away again in its hiding place.

She didn't think of it at all as a trick or a stunt for public display, or even as a part of Orbit's never-ceasing education. Nothing like that. It was something she would do some day for herself alone. She would simply bring Orbit into the house and let him see the place in which she spent so many hours away from him. In some obscure way it would be a completion, the closing of a circle, the resolving of a musical chord. There was no logic about it, no common sense, and it was important to nobody but Melanie Webb.

Now though, because of her own stupidity, it seemed to be important to practically everybody. And because of that it was ruined.

Not even the thought that school would be over for the summer in just two more days now served to lighten these melancholy reflections. Neither did the news with which Mom greeted her when she got home. She would have to go, Mom told her regretfully but firmly, for a final fitting of the dress she was to wear to Diane's graduation, just a week away. Furthermore, she would have to take Diane's own dress, which needed some minor changes.

Melanie protested, but merely as a matter of form, knowing the distasteful errand must be done. It was distasteful because the dressmaker was Mrs Griswold, an ageing widow of such iron-clad respectability that her very presence filled Melanie with all manner of improper impulses.

'I know she's an awful bore,' Mom said, 'and I do wish she could get through a whole sentence without stuffing a platitude into it, but this chore's got to be done.'

Melanie shrugged resignedly. The afternoon couldn't be much more dismal than it had already been. 'At least I can ride Orbit over and back,' she said, 'so the whole time won't be wasted.'

Orbit did no more than roll a reproachful eye when Melanie hooked the string of the big dress-box over the saddlehorn and let the box hang down against his shoulder where he knew it was sure to bump when he moved. The time had been when such a cumbersome, unwanted, off-balance burden would have turned him into a whirlwind of fright and fury, but now it was no more than a minor nuisance. One by one, over the months and years of his training, Melanie had hung all manner of things from his saddle – from horrible clattery things like clusters of pots and pans to heavy, awkward things like big sacks filled with sand. He didn't like them and never would, but as long as Melanie was around to reassure him he would tolerate them. The point was to prepare him to carry any sort of load, even though he might never be called upon to do so.

The same principle had applied in his road training, an important project which had called for Pop's help. First Pop had brought the car into the pasture and driven it around as slowly and quietly as possible while Melanie controlled Orbit and got him used to the idea of this strange mechanical monster. Gradually Pop made the car noisier and noisier, racing the motor and blowing the horn. On succeeding days they went out on the road at the hour just after dawn when no other cars were around, and went through the same procedure. The final step was for Pop to change to the pick-up truck he used in his work. Filling its steel bed with tools of all sorts, pieces of old metal, round rocks, and anything else that would roll and bounce around, he went clattering and banging up and down the road while Melanie rode Orbit steadily along its right shoulder. For a week of mornings he sweated and quivered and jumped, his ears laid flat against his head in a passion of anger and fear. Then gradually he calmed. At the very end Pop behaved like a madman, zooming suddenly round curves with a horrendous din, squealing his tyres, roaring alongside in low gear at full throttle, leaning on the horn and yelling a warwhoop at the top of his voice.

Pop ruefully told somebody later, 'I should have been arrested fifty times. I'm a nervous wreck; I'll have to buy a new pick-up, and all the neighbours are convinced I ought to be locked up. But, by George, Mellie has sure got a steady horse!'

It was true. Melanie could ride him anywhere – even in parades with brass bands hooting and blaring right behind him, clowns dashing around making sudden movements and strange noises, and applauding crowds lining the streets.

Mrs Griswold lived in a sprawling old house in Wilby, a tiny village that would have been called a suburb of Cascade if Cascade had been big enough to have suburbs. It consisted of about a dozen houses and a little grocery store with two red petrol pumps in front of it, and the only hitching-rail in the whole area surviving from the long-gone days.

This one was a real convenience for Melanie, because Mrs Griswold lived just two houses from the store and didn't want Orbit standing around on her lawn. 'Horses are so *untidy*, dear,' was her stuffy way of putting it. Anyway, it was a good idea to tie him where he was out of her sight. Everyone who lived in Wilby knew enough to leave him alone, but it was always possible that a stranger might happen along and feel an urge to pet the pretty horse, not knowing that the pretty horse detested being petted by anyone but Melanie.

Knotting the reins to the rail, she braced herself for the ordeal and walked up to Mrs Griswold's door.

53

Fortunately, it was never necessary to talk much in the dressmaker's presence beyond making polite noises from time to time. Mrs Griswold's sole and abiding interest was other people, which seemed strange because apparently there weren't any people she approved of, except possibly ministers, and she wasn't always quite sure about even them. Melanie let the words flow through, above, below, and around her, responding with the proper motions when told to lift her arms, turn this way or that, or hold still.

She emerged at last to find Orbit peacefully dozing at the hitching-rail, gave him a slap on the neck in passing, and went into the little store for an ice-cream bar to take the taste of Mrs Griswold out of her mouth.

Mr Wilby, who had been running the store for as long as anybody could remember, seemed almost incredibly old. The son of the pioneer Wilby who had founded the town, he was small – scarcely taller than Melanie herself, but amazingly wiry and quick. From his wrinkled face with skin as thin as paper, shone a pair of eyes as blue as forget-me-nots and as full of merriment as a boy's.

When Melanie came in, he looked up from his copy of *The Western Farmer*, spread out as always on the glass top of the candy counter, and smiled. In spite of his false teeth, which no longer fitted well, his smile held the radiance of a spot of sun on a far-off hill. 'Now here *is* a happy surprise!' he said, his high voice only the least bit quavery. 'Is all well with you, Little Miss?'

'Fine, thank you, Mr Wilby,' Melanie said. He knew her name, but he never called her anything but Little Miss, and because he was Mr Wilby she didn't mind.

She started on the ice-cream, then decided to have a Coke too. Listening to Mrs Griswold for almost an hour was thirsty work. Then she found herself telling Mr Wilby all about her day in school and the plan for taking Orbit into the house. She felt a little silly, bringing the whole thing out into the open, but it didn't seem to matter. Because of Mr Wilby's great age, it was more like writing in a diary than talking to another human being. She concluded, rather lamely, 'I know it's a silly thing, and I really shouldn't do it.'

Mr Wilby's eyes seemed even a brighter blue as he looked at her. 'Bet your life it's silly,' he said promptly, 'but you're bound and determined to do it – I can see that. So do it with an easy mind.' He climbed up on his high stool behind the candy counter and went on. 'Tell you something, Little Miss. I'm ninety-four years old – a mighty long time to be around this world. And I've got many a regret, many a thing I'd do different if I had the chance, or not do at all. But you know what I regret the most? The things I *didn't* do. Crazy things that I'd have got pleasure out of but didn't do for fear of being laughed at.' He chuckled dryly. 'Laughed at by folks I've outlived a lifetime.' Then he grew sober, staring hard at Melanie. 'You've got a head on your shoulders, Little Miss. You'll always have it. But you won't always be young and pretty as a picture and full of fancies like you are now. And those fancies are important. *Use* 'em. If I've learned anything at all in near a hundred years, it's that folks should do whatever they're moved to do in this life, so long as they don't hurt other folks.'

His gaze had wandered towards the front window as he talked, and now he broke off suddenly, 'Hey! Fella out there and he's – '

Orbit! Melanie didn't even think, or tell herself to move. She simply moved. Before Mr Wilby could finish his sentence she banged her Coke bottle down on the counter and leaped to the door.

At the hitching-rail a man stood facing Orbit, his back to the store. Orbit's head was lowered and she could see only the top of it, but by the slight movement of his ears she could tell he was chewing. The man was feeding him something!

Her impression of the man was fleeting – a broad-brimmed hat, a muscular back squeezed into a Western-style shirt, whipcord pants and scuffed high-heeled boots. Her first emotion was amazement, the next was blind, unthinking anger. In her world there was no greater sin than to feed another person's horse without being asked to. It was like spanking the child of a total stranger.

Without a thought as to what she might be getting into, she dashed out of the store and across the stretch of bare ground in front, grabbed the man's arm with both hands and yanked with the strength of outrage.

Unprepared, the man staggered sideways, half turning. Melanie caught sight of a broad tanned face with sun-bleached eyebrows and a grimace of surprise and heard a short, angry word. Then things happened so fast they were like a blur before her eyes.

Because the man was in front of him, Orbit hadn't seen Melanie coming, and when violent action erupted before his very eyes, he threw his head up, snorting explosively. As he did so the knotted reins snapped taut, jerking at the bridle that held him, and he reared in sudden fright, shattering the calm of the early evening with his shrill, spine-chilling call. The rawhide bridle held, but something had to give to the heave of his mighty forequarters.

Melanie heard a crack like a rifle shot and saw the hitching-rail – an eight-foot length of peeled fir log – splinter and break like a stick of kindling across a knee. As the broken ends parted, the reins came free and Orbit was loose, reared high, his forelegs slashing at the air above where the rail had been.

Instantly, the man and everything else vanished from Melanie's mind, and she moved instinctively. Stepping over the broken rail ends, she looked up at the huge body looming above her and spoke clearly and commandingly, 'Ho, boy! Ho!'

Down he came, still confused, still torn by conflicting impulses to run, to lunge, to rear again – but the sound of her voice had reached him. She felt the ground shake under her feet as his hoofs struck it, and she reached out, as calmly as if

56

the whole thing had been an act carefully rehearsed, and closed her hand over the dangling reins. 'Ho, boy!' she said again, just to make sure he knew she was there and everything was all right. 'Now stop acting like a great big baby.' He stood still, trembling a little, his nostrils flared wide.

Remembering the man, she turned, but before she could think of what to do or say a new figure appeared on the scene. It was Mr Wilby. He popped out of the doorway of his store and advanced with funny little hurrying steps. Upraised in one small fist was the wooden-handled iron crank that he used to raise and lower the old green awning above the store window. His voice was shrill with rage, but his words were clear.

'You touch that little girl again, you big ugly murdering baboon, and so help me I'll beat the brains out of you! You leave her alone, you hear me!'

Suddenly one of those never-expected lumps came swelling up in Melanie's throat and her eyes turned hot and misty. Fortunately she was simultaneously assailed by an urge to burst into laughter at the thought of tiny Mr Wilby doing anything at all to the brawny young man who stood between them.

Managing to keep both tears and laughter out of her voice, she called out, 'It's all right, Mr Wilby, it's all right! He didn't do anything to me. I jumped on *him*!'

But Mr Wilby was beyond hearing. He came scuttling on, brandishing his weapon, the fire of battle in his eye. 'You dad-burned gangster – knocking little girls around. Let's see how you stand up to a *man*!'

Melanie could see that he had every intention of swinging at the stranger's head as soon as he got close enough. She had no objection to seeing the man get whacked, but she suddenly remembered that strokes and other dire things happened to old men who got over-excited. '*Please*, Mr Wilby!' she called in alarm. 'Please! I'm all right. He didn't even *touch* me!'

This time she got through to him. Mr Wilby came to a halt, muttering, and the stranger found his voice. 'That's right, gran'dad,' he said with false friendliness, 'I didn't even know she was around.' He turned to Melanie with a smile that was supposed to be ingratiating. 'I didn't mean no harm, girlie. I was just givin' that stud of yours a little handful of oats. I'm downright fond of horses.'

At the word 'girlie' Melanie turned as rigid as Mr Wilby's awning crank. She was trying to think of something devastating to say when Mr Wilby, whose hackles were still up, did it for her. 'If you're so ever-loving about horses, mister, how come you don't know enough not to feed one that isn't your own? You're a phoney, that's why, and I don't like the look of you. So if you're not out of sight in just one minute I'm going to call the law and give oath I saw you hit this little girl. We'll see if you can phoney your way out of *that*. Now git!'

The stranger grinned insolently. 'Don't hanker much for your company neither, gran'dad.' He looked at Orbit, who was standing quietly now, and sighed as if with great emotion. 'Yes sir,' he said, 'real fine chunk of horseflesh you got there.'

Melanie turned her head away, feeling as if he had said something dirty. The stranger thrust his hands into his tight pockets and sauntered off down the road to where a car was parked just a little beyond Mrs Griswold's house. Melanie watched him go, giving the car a mere glance. Then she stiffened and looked at it again. Behind the car, an abused-looking Chevrolet, was the rounded top of an enclosed horse trailer. She didn't actually think about the trailer, though, until later. What had caught her eye was the licence plate on the car. It wasn't the blue and gold of Oregon, nor the black and yellow of California; it was red and white. She narrowed her eyes and, though she couldn't be sure at that distance, she thought she could make out the name 'Nevada'.

Chapter 6

MELANIE arrived home barely in time to wash for dinner. She was bursting to tell Mom and Pop about her encounter with the stranger, but it quickly became apparent she wasn't going to have a chance. The house was oddly silent and as she rushed up the stairs she met Diane. Melanie said 'Hi' but got no answer as her sister went on down the stairs.

One glimpse of her face told Melanie that something was terribly wrong. It wasn't what Katie called Diane's 'going-down-with-the-ship' look – a mask set in tragic lines for the purpose of dramatizing something that didn't really matter. This time she looked truly stricken, and Melanie went about her hand-washing and hair-straightening as quietly as possible, as though somebody in the house were very ill.

Before she had finished, Katie came into the bathroom, closing the door carefully behind her. She looked almost frighteningly solemn. 'Poor Diane!' she said, keeping her voice low. 'And poor Pop! Oh golly, I don't know which to feel sorrier for!'

'What – what *is* it?' Melanie's words came out in a hoarse whisper.

'Diane can't go to Hills College after all! Pop just now told her and – and it darn near killed him.'

For a moment Melanie could only stare. Then she burst out, 'But why? She was accepted and – '

'Money!' Katie broke in harshly. 'Oh blast! Why does everything have to depend on *money*? And all because Pop's so darn nice and *trusts* people. And then they turn round and *rob* him!'

'Rob him?' Melanie echoed.

Katie took two steps and turned back, which was as close as she could come to pacing in the tiny room. 'Mom just now

59

told me about it – and it's *criminal*. These people owe Pop a lot of money. He built a store building or something for them, and he's been trying and trying to get the money because he needed it for Diane. And today the people went bankrupt! He's got to hire a lawyer and file claims and all that, and he may never get a dime, and even if he does it'll take months. And anyway, the best he can do is send her to State because it's a lot cheaper, and then pretty soon there'll be *me* to educate too, and then you, and – oh, what's the use!' She jerked the door open and started out, then turned back obviously calming herself down a little. 'Mom told me to tell you about it so you'd know why everybody's so gloomy and wouldn't accidentally say something to make things worse.'

'Don't worry,' Melanie told her. 'I doubt if I'll be able to say anything at all.'

On the contrary, it seemed to Melanie afterwards that she had done nothing but talk during the interminable dinner. Pop look haunted, as if he had committed some shameful crime, while Diane tried courageously to look as if nothing had happened. The combination spurred Melanie, much to her own surprise, to try to fill the conversational vacuum single-handedly.

She rattled on, talking about everything, or almost everything, that came into her head. She talked about what she and Orbit were going to do in the big show in August. She related the story of her encounter with the stranger and was nearly at the end of it when Diane pushed back her chair, stood up, and said in a muffled voice, 'Excuse me.' Her dark eyes, softly glinting with tears, turned briefly on Melanie. 'Thanks, Mellie, for trying,' she said, then left the room, half running.

The long silence that followed was broken by Katie, who said, 'Oh, blast it all!'

'Katie!' Mom reproved automatically, but her heart wasn't in it. Pop unconsciously heaved a loud sigh.

As for Melanie, aimlessly shoving a lone green bean around her gravy-smeared plate, there was nothing to be seen but more problems. There were her own problems, of course, the unpleasant stranger for one, and her rash promise to the tiresome Conrad for another. But these were trivial in comparison with the disaster of the money and Diane's education.

Melanie had never given much thought to college. She merely assumed that some time in the misty future she would go to one because it was the thing to do. For Diane, though, there was nothing misty about it. It was right now. She had had her heart set on Hills for as long as Melanie could remember hearing anything about it. In spite of what Katie called, blightingly, its 'snob appeal', it was undoubtedly the finest college for girls in the West, and Diane, though not a natural student like Katie, had worked hard in high school to keep her grades up to the Hills' standard. And now, because of this monstrous unfairness, she couldn't go at all.

Then there was Katie. In only one year she too would be going off to college. Though two years younger than Diane, she was only a year behind in school because she had skipped one of the early grades. She would have skipped another if a school rule hadn't stood in the way. To Melanie, Katie was just Katie – big, funny, almost pretty, and much loved – but she knew her sister's classmates called her 'the Brain'. Even Mom had said once, only half joking, that, 'Katie's so bright she scares me sometimes. She makes me think my brain must be about the size of a raisin.'

And Katie too had a college of her dreams. It was one of the big ones in the East. She didn't talk about it much, but when she did a sort of light appeared in her animated eyes. Katie, of all people in the world, Melanie thought, deserved the chance to go to whatever college she chose. Unlike Diane, or Melanie herself, Katie loved to learn things for their own sake. But what if there weren't enough money to send her . . .

Shocked by the thought, Melanie raised her eyes to her sister, who at that moment was sneaking a compassionate look at Pop. Pop in turn put an end to the uneasy silence by getting up abruptly, forcing a rueful smile. 'Well,' he said, 'I

61

guess we won't get anywhere sitting around avoiding each other's eyes.' He looked at Mom. 'Why don't you and I go out for a little drive?'

'Which means,' Katie said, trying for the humorous touch, 'why don't you go and talk where there aren't a lot of large adolescent ears around.' She stood up in one of the quick, graceful movements that were always surprising in so large a girl. 'You go on, Mom. Mellie and I will clean up.'

While Katie washed and Melanie dried, both were unusually silent for a long time. At last Melanie said, feeling a little ashamed of her ignorance, 'What *does* it cost to go to Hills?'

Katie answered promptly. 'Pretty close to twenty-five hundred dollars, counting everything.'

Doing her arithmetic out loud, Melanie said, 'Four years. That's six hundred dollars a year. No wonder Pop – '

Katie choked off a snort of laughter. 'It's that much a *year*, Mellie. *Now* do your arithmetic.'

Standing motionless, aghast at the monstrous figure of ten thousand dollars, Melanie said at last, humbly, 'I just didn't have any idea. I'm just plain stupid.'

To her astonishment Katie's reply was an almost violent outburst. '*You're* stupid! What about me? You didn't know about the cost, but *I* did! And I went right on thinking I could go jaunting off to Columbia or any other university I took a fancy to, the same as if Pop were a millionaire! How's *that* for stupidity?'

Melanie found she was wiping an already dry plate over and over, staring at her sister. Then she in turn burst out, 'But Katie! You've dreamed and planned about going there! You've worked out all the things you're going to study. You've – Katie, you've *got* to go there!'

'*Got* to!' Katie controlled herself with an effort, then went on, a little too calmly. 'What I've *got* to do, Mellie, is just what millions of other kids have *got* to do when they don't have rich men for fathers. I've got to do the best I can with whatever money there is.' She dropped a handful of silver-ware into the dishpan and scrubbed away at a fork. ' "The Brain" of Cascade High School,' she said ruefully, 'has been living in a dream world, and it's time she woke up. I was operating on the theory that everything would work out the way I wanted it to just *because* I wanted it to. Well, that isn't the way the world operates. I knew it all the time, but I wouldn't face up to it. But, Mellie, everybody's got to face up to it sooner or later. Look at Diane. She's having to do it right now. And if she can do it, so can I. So that's what I'm – '

'No, Katie, no!' The words poured out of Melanie almost of their own accord, giving her no time to wonder why she felt so strongly, why it was so unthinkable to her that the extraordinary Katie should have to make do with an ordinary education. 'You *do* have to go East and study to be a – what-ever that was. You can do something great. Everybody says so! Katie, you've got to go and do those things, even if I have to – '

She bit off her words, shocked to the very bones by the appalling thing she had been on the brink of blurting out.

Mercifully, at that moment the telephone rang in the front hall and Katie hurried to answer it. Melanie stood frozen, still holding the plate she had dried long since. She was alone in a terrible stillness, and even though she fought against it her mind went on with all the relentlessness of the Gigi dream and finished her sentence for her. '. . . *even if I have to sell Orbit.*'

The sound of Katie's returning steps jerked her out of her paralysis and she started putting dishes away with more noise than necessary.

'That was Dear Eddie,' Katie said. Glancing up, Melanie saw to her immense relief that her sister's eyes were alive with their 'friendly fiend' expression. Whoever Eddie was, Melanie was grateful for his timely call. Things had been much too serious for much too long.

'Who's Dear Eddie?' she asked.

'One of Diane's mooncalves. She *loathes* him. Anyway, I knew she wouldn't want to talk to anybody now.'

Hanging up the dish towel, Melanie said, 'I suppose you said something awful to him.'

'Me?' said Katie, pretending offence. 'I only said she couldn't talk to anybody because she'd taken a vow of eternal silence.'

Melanie was still laughing when Mom and Pop suddenly came in the back door. Mom hurried on through the kitchen with no greeting but a brief smile, but Pop stood in the doorway, filling it up. Melanie was pleasantly surprised to see that, while he didn't look exactly happy, he no longer wore the stricken look of a mere half hour ago.

He smiled at the two pairs of eyes that were fastened on him. 'Mom and I didn't pass any miracles,' he said, 'but we did come up with a sort of minor inspiration. It's like putting a band-aid on a broken leg, I guess, but at least it's something. Something to take your sister's mind off – off her troubles.'

His eyes clouded a little. 'I'm afraid you two are going to be the fall guys in this little scheme.'

'Fall guys?' repeated Melanie, who had never heard the term.

'The victims,' Katie interpolated. 'The sacrificial lambs. Go on, Pop. What do we have to do – open a couple of veins and bleed for a noble cause?'

'Worse than that,' Pop said. 'You've got to stay home while the rest of us go to San Francisco for a week.' He hurried on apologetically, while Melanie and Katie exchanged startled glances. 'This just seemed the right time. We'll kill three birds with one stone. Your mother's been wanting to visit your aunt for about three years now, and I've kept putting her off. And Mr Bristow's been after me to go down there and confer with a sculptor who's going to do a lot of the panel work for Bristow's house. Matter of fact, he wants to pay my expenses. I didn't see how I could spare the time, but – well – Mom thought a round of shopping in the big city would do wonders for Diane's morale, and – '

64

'Pop, it's a terrific idea!' Katie broke in. 'And don't worry about Mellie and me. I don't care one way or the other, and you probably couldn't pry *her* loose from Orbit for a whole week, and we'd practically double the expense, so everything's lovely. When are you going?'

'Next week, right after Diane's graduation,' Pop said, looking so relieved at this ready acceptance of his plan that Melanie felt a twinge of guilt. The twinge resulted from the fact that her first thought had been that a week with Mom and Pop away was made to order for such a project as bringing Orbit into the house.

Orbit, in contented ignorance that fate was meddling with his future, emerged from a half doze with a start a little later when he saw Melanie making her way towards him across the pasture. He was standing in the far corner where the Hansens' fir grove cast a long, deep shadow in the rays of the setting sun.

He greeted her with a gentle nicker and she regarded him sombrely for a time before she spoke. 'You big old monster. You don't know how lucky you are just to be a horse.'

What she meant, though it was far too complicated to put into words, was that a horse needn't think about anything at all beyond whether or not his stomach was comfortable and the flies weren't too persistent. When something threatened him he faced a simple choice: He could fight, or he could run away. And if he chose to run he could do so with a pure, untroubled mind. No nagging, hateful voice would whisper in his ear. 'Coward! Weakling!'

Melanie, who couldn't run away because running away from a thought was impossible, had chosen to fight, and because her mind was quick she had a great many weapons to fight with.

One of them was that it was ridiculous to think she could sell Orbit for anywhere near enough to help Katie go to the school of her dreams. But this weapon quickly blunted itself against the nagging suspicion that Orbit would bring a great deal of money indeed. She remembered what Pop had said once: 'Anything is worth exactly what somebody is willing to pay for it.' Though she tried not to, she couldn't help remembering the things Mr Bristow had said, or hinted at. It was obvious that he, for one, would be willing to pay a lot.

Then there was the quite reasonable thought that her sisters' problems were their own, not hers. Their education wasn't her responsibility, and nobody in his right mind would say it was.

And so the battle went, one side gaining the edge, then losing it to the other, and the battlefield was littered with the bodies of slain arguments. It was a wearying battle, and in the thick of it Melanie stepped past Orbit to the fence and dropped to the grass.

The bitter struggle resolved itself at last into a kind of frantic stalemate. She had to do this unthinkable thing – and yet she couldn't! Life without Orbit was a bleak grey desert stretching sullenly on and on to a joyless infinity.

She was in the midst of picturing this dismal prospect when Orbit, growing increasingly disturbed that she should sit so long and so silently, lowered his head, and with his silken nose gave her a gentle nudge.

Orbit's gentle nudges being what they were, Melanie went sprawling sideways to the grass, but she whirled, flung an arm around his neck, and with a wild sort of laugh let him jerk her to her feet as he raised his head.

She clung there for a long moment, her face buried in his smooth, warm neck. Her tears, in turn, felt warm on his skin, and he rolled his eyes back in a useless attempt to see what she was up to now.

Soon she loosed her hold, tugged a handkerchief from a pocket and blew her nose defiantly. Then she grasped the bony curve of his jaw and tugged. 'Come on,' she said. 'Let's saddle up and go over to see Baldy.'

At the Penfield place she found Ritchie in the kitchen eating a late supper. 'I've been cutting hay all evening,' he explained. 'All this sunny weather, it ripened early this year. Sit down and have some pie while I finish up.'

Declining the pie, Melanie sat down. 'I'll just watch.'

'Big treat,' Ritchie said, grinning with his mouth full. 'Well, what's new over your way?'

This was a tactful way of asking why she had come over, and Melanie hesitated, knowing quite well why she had come. It was to lay the whole awful problem in front of Ritchie and to ask his advice. But now, looking at Ritchie's square and rather dirty face, and his steady blue eyes, she knew she couldn't do it. She knew it because all at once she saw herself as a cheat and a fraud. She didn't really want his advice; she merely wanted him to tell her not even to dream of selling Orbit. She was sure he would. And why? Because she had no intention of telling him the strong, compelling arguments for selling Orbit but only the weak ones that were easily disposed of. She was going to tell him the truth, but only part of the truth, and that could amount to the same thing as a lie.

Annoyed with herself for carrying honesty to such fantastic lengths, she quickly cast about for something else to say. 'This afternoon,' she said, 'it was my turn to run into that phoney horse trader of yours.'

Ritchie glanced up, his face alert. 'What happened?'

She told him the whole story while he finished a meal that included two pieces of pie and what looked like a gallon of milk. Then he tilted his chair back. At last he said soberly, 'Did you tell your dad about it?'

'Of course.'

'What did he say?'

'Nothing,' she answered truthfully, not explaining that, considering Pop's state of mind at dinner, she could have told him about a murder and got no reaction.

'Well,' Ritchie said, looking doubtful, 'if he isn't worried about it, I guess there's no reason – '

'Worried about it!' Melanie broke in sharply. 'Why in the world should he be worried about it?' She knew she was welcoming the chance to argue with Ritchie, but she went ahead anyway. It would be such a lovely relief from arguing with herself.

'I already spotted him for a phoney,' Ritchie said, looking vaguely troubled. 'And now I can't imagine why he wants to go around feeding oats to strange horses.'

'Oh, he just doesn't know any better, silly! Lots of people don't. They – '

'Mellie, *this* guy knows better!' Ritchie's chair came down with a thump and he leaned forward earnestly. 'Did you notice his boots?'

'For heaven's sake, what do his boots have to do with anything?'

Ignoring this outburst, he pursued his subject. 'Those boots have seen a lot of wear – and not just pounding sidewalks either. And I saw a couple of little round dents right below the ankles. Mellie – that guy usually wears spurs – and *uses* them!'

'Spurs!' Melanie gasped, horrified. In her world the use of spurs on a horse was little different from using a whip to train a child. Spurs, when they weren't worn just for show, meant hard riding – stunting – rodeo. They meant the kind of riding that drove a horse – through pain or the fear of it – to perform feats beyond its strength, endangering its safety and even its life.

After she had time to think about it a little, though, she said, 'But Ritchie, I still don't see what sense it makes. What has it got to do with *me*?'

'Darned if I know – but I'm going to keep my eyes open.' Ritchie got up. 'Right now, come and have a look at my hay.'

'How can I?' Melanie said practically, looking towards the window. 'It's dark out.'

'Moonlight,' he said. 'And anyway all you have to do is smell it.' He grinned. 'It smells like money. Come on.'

68

Half an hour later, as they rode along the moonlit road, Ritchie was still talking about hay and the money it would make him. He had insisted on riding half-way home with her. She listened amiably with part of her mind, content to have something going on besides her own dreary thoughts. She knew that Ritchie's father, who had given up farming because of his heart and taken a job in town, had made Ritchie a deal they were both proud of. Ritchie rented the equipment and the sixty acres from his father, and whatever profit he made was his own.

He was rambling happily on. 'With what I make from my own hay and then from cutting and baling other people's, I should make pretty close to five hundred dollars by the middle of July. With what I've got saved it'll be darn near enough for my first year at college.'

Melanie came crashing back to reality. That word again! Didn't anybody in the world ever talk about anything but college?

Unaware of having said anything disturbing, Ritchie went on with the monologue which he apparently mistook for a conversation, and all unknowing uttered the words that were to seal the fate of the girl and the horse beside him.

'Gee,' he said, heaving a regretful sigh, 'if it wasn't for my kid sisters I could maybe even go to Caltech.' He turned towards her and she could see his grin by moonlight. 'Girls, you know. They're expensive.'

Melanie had a strong feeling she didn't want to hear about it, but she couldn't just sit there like a lump. 'What have your sisters got to do with it?'

Apparently he didn't catch the sharp note in her voice, for he went on in the same regretful tone. 'Oh, you know how it is. Pop hates to admit it, but he needs the rent I pay him. And it's only fair because he could always rent to somebody else. He even offered to waive it, so I could try for Caltech. That's the best engineering school there is. But – oh, well – no use talking about it.'

69

'Oh, don't be so disgustingly *noble*!' The words burst out and then seemed to hang in the quiet night air like smoke. Appalled at herself, she had no idea why she had said them, except that suddenly everything had seemed to close in on her. She knew now what her decision about Orbit must be. She felt

trapped, and for that brief moment innocent Ritchie was to blame, and she had lashed out at him.

She heard his saddle creak as he turned to stare at her and was grateful for the darkness that hid his expression from her. 'Oh Ritchie,' she said quickly, 'I'm sorry! *Really* sorry! That was a *stinky* thing to say, and you didn't deserve it any more than – than Baldy did. It's just that I'm all screwed up. Some time I'll tell you about it – but not now.'

'It's all right, Mellie.' His voice was quietly comforting. 'I had a feeling all along you were sort of – sort of upset. And you don't need to ever tell me about it if you don't feel like it.' He paused, then hurried on. 'Hey, you going to come watch me play in the All-Star game Saturday?'

Melanie felt a grateful smile at her lips. 'Baseball!' she exclaimed, obliterating the same as witheringly as she could manage. 'Ritchie, I've got news! My folks are going to take Diane to San Francisco for a week. And you know what I'm going to do while they're gone?'

She babbled on, telling him about Conrad and all the rest of it. Ritchie made appreciative comments and laughed in all the right places. After he and Baldy had turned at the top of the hill and headed back, she was able to ride the rest of the way almost as calmly as if the world had not stopped turning and a future still lay ahead.

Chapter 7

THE next day plunged the Webb household into a week of such frenzied activity that Melanie had little time to think about the dreadful decision she had made, or about the stranger who wore spurs. In any case, there was no need to do anything about the decision until there was a chance to get Mr Bristow alone. He turned up three times during the week with some new idea about his house plans, but each time he was on his way somewhere else and in a tearing hurry. Melanie was able to shove her problems into that cluttered corner of her mind where she kept all manner of items she would rather not think about.

The reason for all the turmoil was that preparations for the San Francisco trip had now been added to those for the graduation. Pop was gone every day from daylight to dark, working extra hours to make sure the men of his crew had enough work laid out in advance to keep them busy during his absence. Mom gave up painting and devoted herself to what was, for her, the Hydra-headed task of getting three-fifths of the family ready to go away and two-fifths of it to stay home. In addition to cleaning the house from attic to basement, she made lists of everything. There was a list for Katie and Melanie of telephone numbers to call in the event of every conceivable emergency. The list began with the Sheriff's Office and Fire Department and ended with the dentist and the man who took care of the septic tank. There was a list of menus for well-balanced meals and another for jobs to be done each day. The latter ended with the stern injunction: *Lock all doors at bedtime including garage.* Beneath this was added in pencil, apparently an afterthought: 'Melanie sleep in *bed*, not *barn*.'

Katie's favourite list, which she said ought to be registered with the Library of Congress, was found thumbtacked to the door of the upstairs bathroom.

FRIDAY (Graduation Day)

Upstairs Bathroom Shampoo, Hair-set & Dryer
(in MY Bedroom) Schedule
(Absolutely INFLEXIBLE)

	Bathroom	Hair Dryer
MELANIE	9.00 a.m.	9.45 a.m.
KATIE	9.30	10.30
MOM	10.30	11.30
LUNCH	12.15 p.m.	
DIANE	1.00 p.m.	At discretion but *must* be finished by 5 p.m.

POP – *Downstairs* bathroom *only*   4 p.m.

'What we need,' was one of Katie's comments, 'is a sort of conveyor thing – like one of those three-minute car-wash places. Pay now, dry later.'

All went well with Mom's inflexible schedule on Friday and promptly at 6.30 p.m. the Webb family, hastily fed but flawlessly groomed, was ready to start for the high school. Pop insisted on lining his womenfolk up on the front steps for a picture – with Diane and Katie in the middle and Mom and Melanie at the ends, because they were the smallest.

After Pop snapped his picture he said, 'Hold it!' and stood looking at them with a funny little smile on his face. 'This shot's just for my memory,' he said. 'Gee, you're a beautiful bunch!'

Melanie, who secretly did feel rather beautiful in her hyacinth-blue cotton dress with the petticoats fluffing out its full skirts, felt an oddly maternal sort of affection for Pop.

Katie said, 'You ought to see us with our teeth in,' and Pop had to stop looking sentimental in order to roar with laughter.

At the high school Diane vanished to wherever it was the seniors were gathering, leaving the rest of them with half an hour to dispose of before the ceremony began. Some other parents came up and started talking to Mom and Pop, and a moment later two girls pounced on Katie, both talking at once. Melanie didn't feel neglected, because she wasn't looking for attention, but she did feel a little useless. The wide central corridor of the school was familiar to her, but she found herself looking at it in a new way. It was strange, and a little frightening, to think that this was the place to which she would be coming every day, once the summer was over.

In this mixed mood, she was suddenly startled to hear an all-too-familiar voice and to find herself looking at Conrad Wemmer, right between the ears. She hadn't seen him coming, infuriating grin and all.

'Oh, *there* you are!' said Conrad in the accusing tone employed by all people who say, 'Oh, there you are.'

'Hello, Conrad,' she said with resignation.

Conrad was making violent gestures towards somebody behind him, and in a moment Melanie was confronted by a tall, skinny boy, about seventeen, who appeared to droop under the great burden of his own importance and who carried a large camera with a flash attachment. 'Well, well!' said this apparition, granting Melanie a watered-down smile, 'so this is the Number Three Webb girl!'

Conrad, meanwhile, was babbling away about this being

74

Larry something-or-other who would be editor of the high school paper next year, and who had appointed him, Conrad, as freshman reporter.

Melanie felt her prickles rising like a hedgehog's. She was painfully aware that all conversation around her had come to an unceremonious halt.

Into the middle of this silence, the Larry person dropped a large, ungainly shoe. 'Well, we'll certainly have to have a picture,' he said, 'of the little Webb girl who keeps her horse in the house!'

Melanie felt her whole body turn to solid ice in an instant. If she could have died on the spot, even in extreme agony, she would cheerfully have done so.

Behind her, Pop cleared his throat uncertainly. 'How's that again, young fellow?' he said.

Melanie's wild glance suddenly caught that of Katie, who was staring at her with a look of such intense concentration that her thinking mechanism was almost visible. Then, to Melanie's amazement, Katie's lips curved in the beginning of a smile. A second later she broke into her contagious laugh and looked straight at the Larry person.

'Oh, you – you *idiot*! You've got your facts all backwards – as usual. She doesn't keep her horse in the *house*; it's the other way *around*. She lives in the *horse's* house – in the *stable*. She's got a *bed* out there.'

Larry's aura of importance was melting like wax in a hot sun. The wilting journalist pulled the rags of his dignity about him and made off down the hall with long, loping strides, surrounded on all sides by Conrad, a small, agitated satellite.

As calmly as if nothing at all had happened, Katie turned to Mom and Pop and said, 'Guess we'd better go in and get our seats now.'

Not until they were all seated and the high school orchestra had started playing some sort of graduation-time music was there privacy enough for Melanie to look up at her sister and say with honest admiration and deep gratitude, 'Gee, thanks. You practically saved my life.'

'My pleasure,' Katie said grandly. 'That Larry Bolton gives me internal goose pimples anyway.' She turned to answer some question of Mom's, then looked sideways at Melanie again. 'Let's have this understood: if Orbit's going to live with us, *I* get to use the bathtub before *he* does!'

Melanie choked, and the orchestra broke into the strains of the Processional March.

It was a beautiful ceremony, everybody kept saying afterwards, and Melanie supposed it was, but she couldn't see why it had to be so everlastingly long.

By the time they got home at last it seemed to Melanie it must be almost three in the morning, though it was actually not quite ten o'clock. In her room she took off her finery with a mixture of regret and relief, and got into jeans and a shirt. On her way through the kitchen she ran into Pop, who was removing his tie with an expression of immense satisfaction. 'Well, Cinderella!' he said. 'Back to the peas and lentils?'

Before she could answer, Mom called from upstairs. 'Ben! Hurry up and get out of that suit so I can pack it!'

He called back, 'Coming, Mother!' and winked at Melanie as she hurried out to the barn.

Even before she flipped the switch inside the tack-room door, lighting up the room and the stall beyond, she felt a sharp awareness that something was different. Her eyes moved quickly, taking a swift inventory of the familiar objects all around, and were instantly drawn to a black shapeless mass bulging out on either side of a rafter high above her head. Even as she looked, it moved, and she found herself staring up into the yellow eyes of Musclebound. She felt herself relax with a smile which changed immediately to a puzzled frown, and she voiced her thought. 'What in the world are you doing up *there*?'

The big tomcat unblinkingly regarded her with a baleful

glare, and made no movement to come down from his dizzy and uncomfortable-looking perch. Even at that distance he looked bigger than usual, his fur all fluffed out. Had something frightened him?

Melanie stood irresolutely, looking around. Nothing else was unusual, nothing out of place, and yet . . .

In a flash of knowing, it came to her. Tobacco smoke!

It was so faint that if she had been used to the smell of it – if anybody in her family smoked – she would never even have noticed it. But it was unmistakable. In a flash of movement she was at the tiny window overlooking the pasture side of the barn, making blinkers of her hands to shut out the light of the room behind her.

There in the pasture stood Orbit, a silver statue in the moonlight. His head was up, looking towards her.

Telling herself firmly to stop acting as jumpy as an Arabian filly, she began a minute, painstaking examination of the whole stable, concentrating particularly on the floor. She found nothing but the usual litter of wisps of hay. Going around the partition and into the big box stall, she continued her inspection there.

The floor was covered by a layer of bedding shavings, except for a patch just behind the manger that was scraped bare by Orbit's restless forefeet. At one edge of the bare patch something caught her eye and she squatted for a closer look.

A tiny scrap of paper burned black along one edge and a few yellow-brown shreds of tobacco were all that remained of a cigarette that had plainly been tossed to the floor and ground out beneath the sole of a boot.

That wasn't all. Almost invisible among the nearly-white shavings were several saliva-sticky bits of apple dropped from Orbit's greedy mouth.

Melanie stood up slowly, her mind racing. Everything was as plain as if it had been printed on the floor. The stranger – and she had no doubt that it was the stranger – had used

77

apples, the titbit Orbit loved best, just as he had used oats the other time, to overcome Orbit's instinctive dislike of strangers. Melanie herself hadn't had any apples to feed him for at least a week. The cigarette proved that the man had stood there in the stall for a considerable time – at least long enough to smoke it. Also, he must have known the family was going to be away from home. Perhaps he had even been lurking around when they left.

But why? Why? The answer was not written with the rest of the story. He hadn't meant to do Orbit any harm, or else he would have done it and Orbit wouldn't be standing calmly out there in the pasture now. Why? she asked herself again, and again there was no answer. There was nothing but a fearful little chill running up her back.

Her useless guesswork was interrupted by a soft plop of Orbit's hoofs in the corral. He had got tired of waiting for her to appear and was coming to find out what she was up to. In a moment his forequarters filled the doorway and he stopped, regarding her curiously. Impulsively she threw her arms round his neck and squeezed with all her strength while he snorted gently with satisfaction.

Then she stepped back and looked up at him. 'For once, just this *once*,' she said, 'I wish you could talk!'

After that, because it had to be done, she measured a coffee can full of oats into his box and went to work on his coat with her brushes. It was a much harder job than usual because she felt herself pulled and pushed this way and that by the need to make a decision, a decision that had to be made very soon.

Should she tell Pop all about it? Half of her mind shouted 'Yes'. That way the whole frightening thing would be right in Pop's big, capable hands. He would know exactly what to do, and do it. But the other half raised an equal outcry. To tell him would spoil everything. He wouldn't stir from the place until he had solved the mystery. The trip that he and Mom and Diane were all looking forward to so much would be postponed or, more likely, called off altogether.

At last she made a compromise decision. It was a weak, wishy-washy kind of decision and she wasn't the least proud of it. She would sleep on the thorny problem and make up her mind in the morning.

Chapter 8

IN the morning, Pop's joyful roar of 'hit the deck!' rattled windows all over the house and brought Melanie out of bed in a leap that took her half-way across the room before she was awake enough to realize she wasn't fleeing from fire or some other calamity. Hastily lassoing her rampageous hair with a rubber band and flinging on her dressing-gown, she stumbled down to the kitchen to help Katie get breakfast ready for the others, as they had planned. She actually didn't even remember her problem until she was getting a package of bacon out of the refrigerator. The recollection took her so by surprise that she started to jerk erect, whacked her head on the ceiling of the refrigerator, and yelped 'Blast!' at the moment Katie walked in, robed and barefooted.

'Tut-tut!' said Katie. 'You're really going to have to cut down on the profanity, Mellie. What are you doing in there, anyway, trying to unscrew the volts, or something?'

'Hey, anybody!' It was Pop, yelling from somewhere in the basement. He sounded muffled.

Katie stepped to the basement door and called down. 'Yes, Pop?'

'Ask Mom if she knows where my little battery light with the cord on it is!'

'Okay!' Katie started for the hall door diagonally opposite the basement door, then stopped. 'Mellie,' she said, 'we might as well be efficient about this. I have a notion it's going to be complicated. You go to the foot of the stairs and yell up to Mom does she know where Pop's little battery light with the cord on it is.'

Melanie did as she was told and in a moment Mom called down, 'What little light does he mean?'

'What does he mean?' Melanie called to Katie.

80

'What do you mean?' Katie called down the basement stairs.

'The one you stick into the battery so you can see to fix the car!' yelled Pop.

'The one you stick in the battery so you can see to fix the car,' said Katie.

'The one you stick in the battery so you can see to fix the car,' yelled Melanie.

'What's the matter with the car?' yelled Mom. 'Won't it start?'

Melanie: 'What's the matter with the car?'

Katie: 'What's the matter with the car?'

Pop: '*Nothing*'s the matter with the car! I just want the *light*!'

Katie: '*Nothing*'s the matter with the car.'

Melanie: '*Nothing*'s the matter with the car!'

Mom: 'Then why does he want a light to fix it with?'

Melanie: 'Then why does he want a light to fix it with?'

Diane (from upstairs bathroom): 'What in the world is all the *yelling* about?'

Katie: 'You keep out of this! – Pop?'

Pop: 'Yes? What did she say?'

Katie: 'Nothing that would do you any good. Look, Pop, we don't seem to be getting anywhere. Could you just sort of do without the light?'

There were mumbling sounds from the basement, then Katie and Melanie came back into the kitchen from opposite doors, both looking as pleased as little boys at a cat fight. Katie said, 'Good, rousing way to start the day off. My blood's starting to circulate already.'

The aroma of bacon was filling the kitchen and the eggs were at hand, ready to crack into the skillet, when Mom hurried in, dressed in the grey denim outfit she favoured for car travel, and looking very worried. 'Is Pop going to be able to get the car fixed in time?' she asked.

Melanie and Katie looked at each other and burst into spasms of laughter, to Mom's bewilderment. Katie patted her fondly on the head. 'You just sit down, honey,' she said, 'and we'll fix you a *real* nice breakfast. Everything's going to be *allllll* right.'

They were all so full of anticipation and excitement that Melanie realized she had made her decision without even thinking about it. No matter what happened she couldn't have brought herself to tell Pop about it and spoil the trip for everybody. Besides, if the trip were called off it might ruin the chance to bring Orbit into the house, and this was important because it would be one of the last things she would be able to do with him – ever.

At last the bags and assorted oddments were all stowed in the car and Pop was out on the drive loudly announcing the time at one-minute intervals, while Mom and Diane pelted from room to room, searching for things they didn't think they had forgotten but might have.

At seven o'clock sharp Pop came stamping in and said, 'Hey, are we going on a trip or aren't we? Come *on*, girls! If there's anything you've forgotten, all we have to do is stop somewhere along the line and phone.'

'Better not,' Katie said. 'We won't be here. Mellie and Orbit are going to join the circus, and I'm going to run off with the Fuller Brush man.'

Pop spread his arms in a menacing semicircle and herded everybody out to the drive. Everybody who was leaving kissed everybody who was staying, and as Mom got into the front seat beside Pop she snatched a tissue and dabbed angrily at the corners of her eyes.

'*Really*, Mother!' Diane said from the back seat. 'You're only going to be gone a *week*.'

'You just be quiet!' Mom retorted with unexpected fierceness. 'I've never gone off and left any of you before, and all of a sudden I – just – don't – *like* – it!'

'*Uh*-oh!' Pop said, switching the engine on and making it roar.

'Ben!' Melanie saw Mom's hand close on Pop's arm with a

sort of desperation. 'Ben, you and Diane go on. I'll stay – '

'Not on your life! Good-bye, girls!' Pop's voice was about three times as loud as it needed to be. The tyres squealed as the car swooshed backwards out on to the road and zoomed forwards to disappear behind the fir grove.

Melanie and Katie stood looking after it for a moment, in a sort of daze. A moment later Katie said in an oddly comforting way, 'Come on. It's our turn for breakfast. We'll eat *buckets* of all the wrong things, and have *monumental* stomach-aches.'

They breakfasted heartily – Katie on a can of chili with beans, Melanie on a peanut butter, mayonnaise and banana sandwich, and they both drank ginger beer. While they sat round the breakfast table, luxuriating in their sense of freedom and waiting for the stomach-aches to set in, Katie stretched with unmannerly abandon and said, 'Well, now that your nosy friend Conrad has given the show away, I guess there's no harm in asking. What's the deal about bringing Orbit into the house?'

Melanie did her best to explain, but the more she tried the sillier it all sounded. To make it worse she was assailed by the almost overpowering temptation to blurt out that bringing Orbit into the house had suddenly become tremendously important because it would probably be the last project she would ever undertake with him. She battled the temptation because she knew, with that merciless honesty of hers, that her motive now was the same as it had been with Ritchie. She wanted to be talked out of her decision. It was even worse than with Ritchie, because Katie would not simply talk against the sacrifice of Orbit, she would vociferously refuse to permit it. In that way Melanie would get credit for having thought of the sacrifice without having to sacrifice anything. To do so was tempting, but it was also contemptible, and Melanie could not allow herself, even for Orbit, to sink so low.

Her explanation floundered to a feeble halt with the words, 'Oh, I guess all I really mean is that if I *don't* do it, I'll always wish I had.'

Contemplating her bare toes, Katie nodded judicially. 'I can't think of a better reason. Wouldn't it be absolutely *brutal* to be about ninety years old and to keep thinking about the time when you *could* have brought a horse into the house and *didn't*?' She shuddered at the thought and added, 'Anyway, you can count on me to help. You know, nail the house back together or something.' She got up and took her dishes to the sink, where she began to wash them under the hot-water tap.

Melanie watched her lazily for a moment, all full of peanut butter and bananas and sisterly affection, then suddenly was struck by a feeling of guilt. Thus far the conversation had been exclusively about her affairs, and Katie had mentioned

84

a project of her own. She raised her voice above the sound of running water. 'What are *you* planning to do? Or is it a secret?'

'It won't be for long,' Katie said, also raising her voice. 'I'm going to study Russian.'

'Russian!' said Melanie, still more loudly, just at the instant Katie turned off the tap. She lowered her voice. 'Gosh! What for?'

Katie shrugged. 'Oh, I don't know. Maybe I'll work for the State Department some day, or marry an ambassador. You never know when it may come in handy to know something other people don't. Besides, it'll be fun.'

'It doesn't sound like fun to me,' Melanie said. 'But how will you do it? Just study a book?'

'I've got a teacher. You know Mrs Ramsay, the one who – '

'The one who lives on the houseboat!' Melanie finished delightedly. 'She's wonderful. But, is she Russian?'

'No, silly! But she's furiously educated. Her husband teaches English at Portland State and studies for his doctorate. She was a college teacher, too, before the baby came. They live on the houseboat because it's cheap. Teachers don't make much money, you know.'

Melanie had a sudden practical thought. 'But how will you get there?'

'Pop's pick-up,' Katie said promptly.

'Gee, can you drive that? And did you ask him?'

'Of course I can drive it – and of course I didn't ask him. He might have said no.'

At that moment the phone rang and they both jumped and started towards the front hall. Katie got there first and answered. 'Hello. Oh – hi, Mom. How are things in San Francisco? What? The iron? Oh, *that's* where all the smoke's coming from!'

Melanie could hear the receiver break into what sounded like static, and Katie held it away from her ear, looking fiendish. 'Mellie,' she said, 'would you go to the utility room and see if Mum left the iron plugged in?'

85

Melanie nodded and waited long enough to hear Katie shout into the phone. 'Just a feeble joke, Mom! *Joke!* Nothing's on fire. All is well. Okay – sure – okay. Have a nice trip.'

In the utility room Melanie found the iron not only un-plugged but neatly put away. When she came back she said, 'You know, you shouldn't tease Mom when she's all nervous about going away.'

'I know,' Katie said contritely. 'Something gets into me. Devils, or something. Next time I'll let *you* answer the phone.' She stretched hugely. 'Well, this afternoon I'm going to be useful. This morning I'm going to – '

'Take a bath!' Melanie whooped, and started up the stairs. 'While you're getting clean I'll be getting dirty. I've got stable work to do.'

Chapter 9

DRESSED for work, Melanie ran out to the barn, realizing there was a tremendous amount to do and that a week was really not a very long time after all.

While Orbit ate his morning ration she cleaned the stall, working round and under him with her short-handled rake. Then she went into Pop's workshop to look it over. It was roughly the size of the living-room in the house. A work-bench ran the length of the room on one side, and on the other, beneath a row of shelves and cabinets, stood the table saw and other machinery shrouded in canvas covers. In one corner stood a dozen or so nail kegs, full or partly full. Selecting three that were empty enough to be moved, she dragged them to the middle of the floor to represent furniture. After giving Orbit a brisk work-out, she unsaddled, exchanged the bridle for a halter, gave him a quick rub-down, and was ready for the lesson.

Slapping his glossy neck and letting him snort down the back of her shirt to signify that all was well between them, she said, 'All right, come on. Do a good job and you'll get a mess of carrots.'

She led him around the stall partition, through the tackroom and out of the people-sized door without a pause, observing with satisfaction that while he laid his ears back in disapproval of the procedure he still ducked his head and walked straight through.

The door to the workshop, she knew, would be a different matter. It was something new. The instant he saw he was about to be led through it he would stop, so the thing to do was to tell him to stop a split second before he did it of his own accord. She judged the timing to a hair's breadth, and the moment she set her foot inside the door she gave a quick downward tug on the halter and spoke a forcible 'Ho!' He stopped and she lounged in the doorway, giving him a chance to look over this place he had never seen before.

'Nothing in there to scare you, now, is there?' she said, reassuring him with the sound of her voice. 'So let's go on in and take a look around. Hup!' The command and the tug on the halter as she started confidently into the room took him by surprise and before he had time to think about it he responded automatically and stepped through the door. In the centre of the room she halted him again for more looking around. 'There now,' she said. 'Do you call this work?' Orbit shook his head violently.

'All right, then, let's see if you can look pretty. *Stretch!*'

Without hesitating he stepped forward with his right forefoot, then his left, leaving his back ones where they were. Melanie let go the halter and walked round him, examining him from all angles, the way a judge would do in the ring. He held the stretch like a statue, and she was as proud of him as if he had been in the ring. Then she stepped back to his head. 'Close up!' He took a step with each hind foot, closing the stretch and standing in a normal way. She could have hugged him, but of course she didn't. The time for praises and rewards was at the end of a lesson, not in the middle of it.

'Now.' Melanie took hold of the halter again. 'You see this barrel? It's really a chair, and we're just going to ease round it without bumping it. Get the idea?'

Like Mom at her painting, Melanie could become so utterly absorbed in her work with Orbit that time lost all meaning. Nothing existed but the two of them. Unlike Mom, though, she had no need of alarm clocks to tell her time had passed. Orbit himself was her alarm clock. In subtle ways she could feel his changing moods as surely as if they were her own. First his attention would wander and she would have to snap him back to the business at hand with sharp words. Next she could feel him getting bored and just a bit impatient. After that came stubbornness, when there would be no use working with him. She knew better, of course, than to let him get to that stage, which usually came from twenty to thirty minutes after the beginning of a lesson.

After she had manoeuvred him round all three barrels twice, she was conscious of the first sign. She made him do one more barrel for the good of his soul, then gave him a slap on the neck and said in her brightest, most excited let's-go-on-a-picnic voice, '*Good* boy! How about we go chomp up some carrots?'

Safely back in the barn, perching on the edge of the manger, she fed him the carrots one by one and kept chattering away, just to entertain him. In the middle of this one-sided picnic they both jumped a little as Musclebound suddenly appeared round a corner of the corral door. Orbit, who had merely glimpsed him from the corner of his eye, swung his head round and down for a better look. Melanie, who could see well enough from her perch, said, 'Oh, ugh!' A large fieldmouse drooped from either side of the big cat's mouth.

Orbit watched him curiously, like a dog watching a beetle,

as he stalked across the floor of the stall, making a slight, rather supercilious detour around two hoofs.

At a spot just to the side of where Melanie's feet dangled down from the edge of the manger, Musclebound gathered his hind legs under him, leaped up beside her with the fluid effortlessness of all cats, and dropped down inside. Melanie promptly picked him up and dropped him to the floor on the tack-room side of the manger. 'You can just do your uggy eating down there,' she told him. 'Durned if I'm going to clean up after you when I don't have to.'

He stared grouchily up at her for a moment, then deliberately put the mouse on the floor, and settled down with his legs tucked under him, the mouse about three inches in front of his nose.

Melanie's dark brows drew together in a frown. Looking at Musclebound had made her think about last night, about the cigarette, the stranger, and all the rest of it. She was aware that she had been doing her best all morning not to think about it, but here it was, and though it was barely noon another night was on the way.

Because she had no idea what she was going to do when night did come, she was relieved and glad when she heard a step on the gravel outside and Katie appeared, wearing shorts and sandals, eating a banana and exuding the bouquet of bubble bath. 'Lo, the mighty hunter!' she said as Musclebound's little tableau caught her eye. 'What's he doing – hypnotizing it?' Then she looked at Orbit approvingly. '*That's* what I like to see. *All* carrots should be eaten by horses. Mom called.'

'Again? My gosh, they'll never get to San Francisco!'

'She wanted to know if she'd written down the phone number of the hotel they're going to stay at.'

'She did write it,' Melanie said. 'I was right there!'

'I told her I was having it tattooed on my stomach,' Katie said. 'Poor Mom. She can't get over thinking we're about three years old. And here you and I are probably better able

90

to take care of ourselves than she is herself – especially *you.*'

'*Me?*' Melanie sat up so straight she almost slipped off the edge of the manger.

'Sure, you.' Katie leaned against the door jamb and peeled her banana clear down to the bottom. 'Anyway, Pop thinks so.' She made her voice as deep as she could, trying to imitate Pop. 'You just leave her alone now, honey. For her size and weight that little gal's stronger and tougher than I am – and smarter, too.'

'Oh, for gosh sake!' said Melanie, who felt like blushing, even if this was just Katie talking. 'When did he ever say that?'

'Oh, I don't know – lots of times. That or something like it. For one, when Mom found out he was letting you move bales around and clean out the barn and all that. Or when you and Orbit first started rocketing around the countryside at night in the middle of a rainstorm. And when you started teaching Orbit to jump, out there in the pasture with that hurdle thing. Remember? That time he actually did restrain her – by brute force. I certainly hope you never go in for lion-taming, because Pop will *let* you, and Mom will go into a coma or something.'

Melanie didn't feel much like a lion-tamer – or any other brave and daring soul – at ten that night when she tiptoed out of the house, carrying her boots, and started across the backyard towards the barn. Feeling afraid was bad enough especially when she really didn't know what there was to be afraid of. But now she felt guilty as well, because in sneaking out this way she was both disobeying Mom and deceiving Katie. But she planned to be back in her own bed soon after daylight.

There was no moon tonight because the sky was overcast, and she had to be careful crossing the lawn for fear of bumping into something. The grass beneath her bare feet was cool and soft and a little damp but she was too jumpy to enjoy

91

it. The night was still and windless, and she knew she couldn't have made a sound, yet suddenly the silence was broken, from somewhere out in the pasture, by the soft nicker that meant Orbit knew she was around. There must have been a faint stirring of the air that brought the scent of her to him, and by the time she reached the stable and groped her way inside she could hear the soft thud of his approaching hoofs. The sound made her feel warm inside, no longer alone, and even a little bit courageous.

As she leaned against the door frame, putting on her shoes, she heard his steps come to a halt and smiled into the darkness, knowing what he was doing as well as if she could see him. He was standing with his head and neck inside, the rest of him outside – sniffing, peering, listening, giving himself a chance to whirl and run for it in case something unpleasant were afoot, such as a bottle of medicine or a man with a set of horseshoeing tools.

'Oh, come on in, suspicious!' Melanie said, unconsciously keeping her voice low. 'What do you think I'm going to do – beat you?'

She didn't want to turn the lights on for fear of being seen from the darkness outside. She was reasonably sure nobody was watching, because Orbit was so calm, but there was no use taking a chance. Groping her way, she pulled a thin slab of hay from the bale and tossed it into the manger. He didn't need a thing to eat, but the sound of his rhythmic crunching was a soothing lullaby.

Orbit of course stepped forward instantly to avail himself of this unscheduled snack, and Melanie felt her way to the wide, heavy door behind him and slid it shut. If he were shut in, she reasoned, nobody could get near him without waking her up. Feeling her way back along the manger partition, she crossed to the bunk, got the alarm clock from the shelf above it and by the light of a match, set it for five o'clock. Still in her jeans and shirt, she lay down and concentrated on listening to Orbit's crunching teeth and on not thinking about anything at all. It had been a long day and she was very sleepy.

She might have been asleep, or she might not, there was no way of telling. She was suddenly sitting bolt upright on the edge of the bunk, her heart pounding painfully. Orbit had whirled round in the stall, his hoofs thumping and scraping on the floor. From deep inside him came a low rumbling sound – not the soft nicker that was his call to her, but sharper, more urgent. Then there was no sound but that of his breathing.

Melanie sat motionless, her hands gripping the wooden frame of the bunk, straining her ears and hearing nothing but the hammering of her own heart. After a minute, unable to bear the inactivity any longer, she got up and groped her way to the little window that looked out on to the pasture. Her eyes were accustomed to the darkness now. Just to the left of the window she could make out the dark mound of the shavings pile. Beyond, the rails and posts of the corral fence separated themselves indistinctly from the darkness behind them. Farther still was the fence at the back side of the pasture, but she couldn't be sure whether she could see it or merely thought she could because of knowing it was there.

Straining her eyes and trying doggedly to calm the pounding of her heart, she jumped when Orbit suddenly shifted his feet nervously. With a hopeless, heartsick feeling she told herself over and over again that she had acted like an idiot, a brainless fool, for not telling Pop her secret. And for not telling Katie. *Why* hadn't she told Katie? Whatever silly reason she had given herself for not telling Katie was gone now from her mind. Katie was bigger, older. Katie knew how to handle guns. But Katie was up in the house, asleep.

Suddenly Melanie's heart nearly stopped altogether. Something out there in the dark had moved. A shadow among shadows, out there along the fence.

She felt her muscles tighten, bringing her body erect. She had remembered what she should have remembered all along. Orbit. What need did she have for Pop, or Katie, or guns, when she had at her command nearly half a ton of powerful bone and muscle, teeth that could rip and tear, forefeet that could strike and slash, hind hoofs that could pound and batter? A cry of fear from her could stampede him into violence before which the strongest man in the world would be as helpless as a baby.

Shivering a little – whether at the thought of what Orbit was capable of doing or because of her own fear, she didn't know – she moved carefully along the partition and into the stall, where she spoke to him, very softly, and reached out until she touched the warm, velvety hide of his shoulder. Then she moved up to his head, groped until she found the crack in the door, and put her eye to it. It was no use; she couldn't see anything at all, so she slid her hand up and scratched the spot between his ears where the little topknot used to be, and stood still, waiting and listening. Though her heart was still beating fast she was far calmer than before. Orbit too was listening. His ears were forward. They twitched back, then forward again. He heard something, though she couldn't.

Then she did. A muffled thump, as though someone had jumped, then, very faintly, a slow tread. It came nearer. It was inside the corral fence now. For a weak moment Melanie's panic threatened to return, but she grabbed a tight fistful of mane and stood fast. Whoever it was, let him touch the door, let him open it. . . . She would leap away with a cry of fear, and Orbit would be on him like a thunderbolt.

The footsteps were clear now, and very close. Melanie even thought she could hear the sound of breathing. She herself wasn't breathing at all.

Abruptly the footsteps halted and a bottomless silence closed over, around, and under everything. Not even Orbit, it seemed, was breathing.

Then, sounding to Melanie as loud as the blast of a bugle in the night, a voice spoke, not two feet from the other side of the door, and her legs turned rubbery under her – with disbelieving amazement, with relief. It was the voice of Ritchie Penfield. 'Hey, Orbit – you in there?'

He sounded puzzled, and this struck Melanie as over-poweringly funny. She quickly let go her handful of mane in order to clap both hands over her mouth. No sooner had she done it, though, than a new fear leaped out of the mix-up of her emotions – the fear that Ritchie would come in and find her skulking here like a frightened mouse in its hole. What could she do? She had to hide because Ritchie might have a flashlight. Or he might even turn on the lights.

The moment she reached that decision Orbit reached one of his own. Having discovered that this was only Ritchie, he lost all further interest in the matter and suddenly thought it might be worth his while to sniff around in the manger just once more. There might be a wisp or two of hay that he had overlooked the last time. Accordingly, with Melanie's hand no longer restraining him, he turned and stepped over to the manger. Under cover of this clomping, Melanie scrambled out of the stall, along the partition, and slid under the bunk at the instant the big door rumbled and creaked, sliding back far enough to let Ritchie in without letting Orbit out.

'Hey, Orbit,' Ritchie said, obviously with nothing but his head inside the barn, 'it's me – Baldy's boy.' Ritchie wasn't afraid of Orbit, of course, but he knew enough to give the stallion plenty of warning before stepping into his stall. Then he did step inside, still talking. 'Hey, boy, how come she's got you shut up in here? You sick or something?'

Huddled as far back under the bunk as she could get, Melanie again had to fight the senseless urge to giggle like a five-year-old. She heard Ritchie moving, then the slap of his hand on Orbit's flank.

'Now don't get jumpy. I'm only going to turn this old flash-light on and take a look around.'

95

All at once a faint gleam brought to Melanie's sight the fascinating vista of a few feet of hay-littered floor partially framed by a corner of the old navy blanket hanging down from the bunk above her.

After a little silence Ritchie said, 'You don't look sick to me.' Then he started to whistle softly through his teeth and the light grew dimmer, then brighter, and Ritchie's boots walked by, along with the frayed bottoms of his jeans. He stopped in front of the manger. 'Ah, quit nosing around, you big pig. There's nothing left in there but the smell.' He whistled some more. Then, 'Oh, quit looking at me like that. Here.' There was the familiar sound of tight-packed hay being torn from the bale. 'You tell her I gave you this and she'll beat my brains out, and then I'll beat *your* brains out. See?'

The thought of everybody beating everybody else's brains out was almost too much for Melanie, and she stuffed the corner of her shirt collar into her mouth to choke back the laughter.

The sound of Orbit's happy chewing filled the barn, and Ritchie spoke again. '*I* heard you whooping at old Baldy a while ago. You want to know why he didn't whoop back? Because I was leading him, and I pinched his nose shut. Old Injun trick. Injun. You know, woo-woo-woo-woo!'

Before she could stop it a snort exploded from Melanie's nose, but fortunately at the same moment Ritchie started whistling again and didn't hear the sound. Something began to itch high up on her back where she couldn't get at it without a lot of scrambling around. She lay there, beginning to enjoy herself, thinking how she would repeat to Ritchie some time his entire conversation with Orbit. Better still, she would tell him she had dreamed it all, make a mysterious thing of it . . .

Then something happened that made her know she would never tell him any such thing. It also dried up – instantly – every giggling impulse in her.

What happened was that Ritchie suddenly stopped whistling and said, quite clearly, 'Mellie!'

Melanie didn't have time to adjust to the shock of hearing herself addressed, or to think of an answer to the question: how could he possibly know? There wasn't time because immediately Ritchie said her name again – 'Mel-an-ie', separating the syllables the way a person does who is trying to teach a new word to a child.

She held her breath, having no idea what was coming next. Orbit chewed unflaggingly on. Then Ritchie spoke again. 'Hey stupid! Don't you even know her *name*?'

Melanie let her breath out very slowly, Orbit chewed, and then there was a movement and a slapping sound. Ritchie was patting Orbit's neck. 'Well, anyway,' said Ritchie, 'she's *our* girl, isn't she, boy? Yours and mine.'

For a long time after he had gone at last, Melanie lay wide awake on top of the bunk, hearing and not hearing the occasional lazy swish of Orbit's tail, the thump of his hoofs as he shifted his weight in his sleep, the clattery tick of the old clock on the shelf above her.

She thought she wasn't sleeping at all, but when the clock brought her scrambling to her feet with its merciless jangling she knew that she must have been. It took a few moments of blinking and staring at the soft dawn light at the window to tell her that the night had gone, taking the clouds along. It was a new day.

She stretched lingeringly and sat up. It was a new day, all right, a little newer than most, somehow. Now how could that be? Then she remembered last night. Slowly she smiled and then, catching herself at it, she bounded out of the bunk and thrust her feet into her boots. She wouldn't think about it now; she would think about it later – at some indefinite but delicious time when conditions would be exactly right.

Right now there was something that had to be done. Just then Orbit interrupted her thoughts with a long, rolling, impatient snort. She laughed aloud and threw him a rather skimpy breakfast. 'Serves you right,' she said. '*Some*body's been feeding you most of the night.'

Then she remembered what it was she had to do. She had to go and make her bed look slept in. She ran for the house, and took her smile along.

Chapter 10

IT was the same way the next morning, and the mornings after that. Always something to be done, never time for a delicious moment. Mom's lists were long, and while neither Melanie nor Katie could in justice complain of overwork, they complained anyway. It made their tasks easier.

Orbit's schooling for civilized house visiting, on the other hand, really was hard work, but naturally Melanie didn't complain about that.

And each night, after all the lights had been off for a while, Ritchie came. It was fun, but it was also somehow a little awesome to lie in her bed and try to guess whose call – Orbit's or Baldy's – would first break the night's deep silence, and then to slide off into sleep.

There was another matter that she had no intention of postponing any longer than it took to make sure Orbit was ready, and on Thursday she decided he was ready.

She made the announcement at breakfast, feeling rather portentous about it. 'This,' she told Katie, 'is the day!'

'Uh-huh,' said Katie, who was of course reading at the table now that Mom wasn't around to stop her.

'Katie! I said this is the day! Today I'm going to bring Orbit into the house!'

'Oh!' Katie said, rejoining the world with a start. 'Jolly good show! Shall I ring up the press?'

'Press? Oh, Conrad. No, we'll have him tomorrow. This is just the dress rehearsal.'

'All right, I'll get dressed.'

By three o'clock that afternoon everything was ready. Every detail that Melanie could think of had been taken care of and she stood in the middle of the living-room frowning in concentration. She had removed the treacherous rug from the front hall and replaced it with a strip of old carpet she found in the basement, fastening it securely to the floor with carpet tacks. A little wedge of wood held the front door open and back against the wall on the chance that it might slam shut behind Orbit and startle him. The telephone receiver was off its cradle so that it couldn't ring unexpectedly. All the alarm clocks that hadn't run down had been silenced. Vases, ashtrays and other breakable items were stowed away in the hall cupboard. Katie had been briefed to keep an eye on the front drive in order to intercept salesmen or anybody else who might feel an urge to ring the doorbell.

As for Orbit, he was as clean as the day he was born, thoroughly exercised, but not weary, hungry but not too hungry, and completely unaware that he was about to be honoured in a manner which seldom in the history of the world had fallen to the lot of a member of his species.

In the kitchen Katie was slicing carrots, potatoes and apples into a dishpan. This was the teatime snack which would be laid before the guest of honour at the dining-room table, which now stood bare of everything but a layer of newspapers. She looked up as Melanie came into the kitchen. 'How about a dollop of mayonnaise?' Katie said. 'It seems a little *inhospitable* just plain.'

Melanie greeted this suggestion with the silence it deserved. She took a very deep breath. Her frown vanished and she smiled. 'Well,' she said, 'here I go.'

But instead of going, she looked at Katie again, feeling oddly shy. 'You know,' she added, 'all of a sudden it isn't just a stupid *job* I've got to do because I said I would. It's like it was the first time I thought of it, a long time ago. It's something I *want* to do, even if it's silly. I'm – I'm all excited.'

Katie put down her paring knife and turned, giving Melanie a strange, intent look.

One of her jokes was coming, Melanie thought, just a shade unhappily. Somehow it didn't seem the time for jokes. A moment later she was fervently telling herself that never again would she underestimate her sister Kathleen. Katie said nothing at all, but took a sudden, unexpected step, put her arms around Melanie, squeezing hard, and kissed her on the cheek.

A second later she was back at the draining-board, a potato in her hand. 'That,' she said, looking firmly at the potato, 'was for my old age.'

Melanie could only stare at her.

'We're going to remember this,' Katie went on, slicing away at the potato. 'All our lives. It's going to be just the way old Mr Wilby told you.' The irrepressible glint came into her eyes. 'We'll click our false teeth and cackle about it. Now go on and get your great big clumsy guest. I'll be dreaming up some party talk to entertain him with.'

On her way out to the barn Melanie found herself in the grip of a strange exhilaration unlike anything she had ever known before. It held an odd admixture of sadness.

When she saw Orbit waiting patiently in his stall there was a quick catch in her throat. He was so beautiful, and he had never belonged to anyone but her . . .

Forcing herself into a mould of brisk efficiency, she led him into the tack-room and got down her new green-and-gold plaid saddle blanket. Securing it to his back with a surcingle, she slipped his show bridle on – the soft black leather one tastefully decorated with little strips and studs of real silver. The guest of honour would be dressed up, even if the hostess wasn't.

The reins in her hand, she led him through the little door, up the lane past the house and into the front yard. Katie was waiting at the front steps, looking idiotic in a frilly white organdie party apron she had dug out of one of Mom's drawers. With her shorts and bare legs the apron looked like some sort of chorus-girl outfit.

When Melanie halted Orbit in front of her she held out her hand graciously and said, 'Star-Wanderer! *My* but it's nice to see you! *Do* come in!'

Orbit sniffed the proffered hand appreciatively. It smelled like carrots and potatoes. But he had to snort a little, too, because there was a lot more of Katie and *it* smelled like bubble bath.

Melanie made a quick hoof inspection, just in case he might have picked up a sharp bit of gravel on the drive. Then she took the reins and peered out towards the road, feeling furtive, like a robber about to enter a bank. It wouldn't do to be seen leading a horse into a house; the story would be all over the county in thirty minutes.

There was no one to be seen. 'Well,' she said, smiling nervously at Katie, 'here we come. You go on in and sort of keep out of the way.'

Katie disappeared, and Melanie reached up and scrubbed Orbit's forehead with her knuckles to put him in a pleasant mood, talking animatedly to prove that nobody was nervous, everything was lovely, and delightful things were about to happen. Then, after a brief pause, she uttered a low but sharp and distinct 'Hup!', snapped the reins taut and stepped through the door as though she hadn't a doubt in the world that once she got inside she would still have a horse along with her.

It worked, as she had known it would. The habit of instant obedience was too much a part of Orbit for him to behave in any other way – unless, of course, something unexpected were to happen.

Something unexpected happened almost immediately.

Since her ears were all but turned backwards like a cat's and her entire mind was concentrated in them, Melanie knew exactly what each of his four feet was doing, though of course she couldn't see any of them. First his right hind hoof clicked on the concrete slab outside the door, then his right forefoot struck with a muffled sound the length of carpet just inside the door. Next the left hind clicked on the concrete and the left fore thumped on the rug. So it went, until all four were on the carpet, still moving obediently forward, and Melanie herself was already through the hall and several steps into the living-room.

That was the point at which the unexpected happened. What Melanie had not once thought of was that a floor with a basement underneath it is not the same thing at all as a floor made of planks laid on hard, unyielding ground. There is a spring to such a floor, though it goes unnoticed by even the biggest human being, and certainly by a ninety-five-pound girl. But when that floor takes the moving weight of nearly a thousand pounds of piano – or of horse – it has to give some-where, and it has to crack and creak a little in the process. Furthermore, the farther the weight moves towards the centre of the room, away from the supporting walls or foundation, the more the floor sags and the louder it protests.

If Melanie's education had included piano moving she would have been aware of these facts and prepared to deal with them. It hadn't, and when her straining ears caught the first faint ominous cracking sound from beneath her feet, her ears, body and voice all reacted with the instantaneous speed of an electric current suddenly switched on in a machine. In far less than a second, the floor cracked, her ear caught the sound and bounced it to her brain, which told her that an un-certain floor would frighten Orbit to an instant halt. Her brain then told her to halt him before he could halt himself, so that he wouldn't think it was his own idea, and at the same moment told her arm and her voice to do the halting.

'Ho!' she said sharply and gave a snap of the reins. Orbit stopped and looked round with an air of faint surprise. She patted his neck and put her brain to work at a less hair-trigger level. Now that she was aware of the problem she knew instinc-tively that the farther Orbit went the shakier the floor would feel to him, and that meant trouble. The hardest thing she had ever done with him – the only battle she had come within a mere gasp of losing to him – was getting him to cross a tiny wooden bridge over a stream down by the river. It had taken more than an hour, worn them both out, and lathered them with sweat, but in the end Melanie had won. He had crossed the bridge. Not in *his* way, either, which would have been by means of a series of frantic, bone-jarring leaps, but in Melanie's way – a dignified and mannerly walk. He still feared and hated bridges, of course, and always would, but he would cross them if she told him to, and that was all that mattered.

This now, was quite another matter. At the bridge there had been plenty of room for his skittish dancing from side to side, his rearing and plunging and fighting the bit. Here there was no room at all. Any undisciplined behaviour would be disastrous.

She could of course back him out the way he had come, give up the whole insane idea. Instantly she rejected the thought. She couldn't give up, not when she had barely started. Melanie was an extremely determined girl, and though neither of them knew it, she had Orbit to thank – at least for a lot of it. But how to proceed from here?

'Great Caesar, but he looks big in here!' Melanie had to control a start as Katie spoke, having actually forgotten there was anybody around but herself and Orbit. Katie was leaning in the archway that connected the living- and dining-rooms, looking rather awed. 'He makes me think,' she went on, 'of a puppet show I saw when I was little. At the end, the man who was working them jumped down on the stage. Scared me to death. I thought he was a giant.'

'Katie,' said Melanie suddenly. 'Go get a couple of carrots.' She had been thinking much too hard to pay attention to anything that was said to her, and was not conscious that she was ordering her sister around.

Katie moved to obey, then looked doubtfully from Melanie to Orbit and back. 'Is there – anything wrong?'

'Not yet there isn't,' Melanie replied, sounding gay and cheerful for Orbit's benefit. 'It's the darn floor. It's going to make him spooky. I can tell.'

Katie said, 'Oh. And carrots will help. I'm on my way.'

She was back in a moment, holding the carrots out towards Melanie. Orbit's ears pricked forward.

Melanie shook her head. 'No, you keep them. I'll explain – and I'll sound like a nut while I'm doing it but don't pay any attention to that. I always talk sort of silly because he likes it and it keeps him nice and calm.'

She chatted away in her high little-girl voice, explaining quickly about the floor and the bridge. She hadn't even finished when Katie's eyes lighted up. 'I get it,' she said. 'And I've got an idea. Why don't you just keep him there while I drag the couch out in the middle. It's a *monster* for weight, and if I get on top of it maybe it'll sag the floor as far as it's *going* to sag. Then you can walk him *around* it.'

'Gee!' Melanie said. 'I never would have thought of that. My carrot idea was ten times as complicated.' She hesitated, glancing at Orbit, who thus far was as relaxed as if he were in his stall, and added, 'Of course, we may have to use *both* ideas.'

Katie went into action. The couch was indeed a monster, custom-built to fit Pop when he was in a 'stretching-out mood' on Sunday afternoons. Heaving and tugging at first one end and then the other, she gradually got it out into the middle of the room. In the process the floor cracked and groaned a time or two, prompting Katie to exclaim triumphantly, 'It's sagging! I *told* you. Beautiful, beautiful sag!'

When the couch was in place, she toppled over backwards and lay flat on the seat, addressing the ceiling. 'There! Me and this old couch, we probably weigh *more* than Orbit.'

A horrible thought struck Melanie. 'Gee!' she said. 'With him and the couch both, do you think the floor will, you know, break through?'

The answer was a peal of laughter, and then, 'You *are* in a state! Pop practically *rebuilt* this house. *Elephants* could play *basketball* in here!'

Reassured, Melanie took a new grip on the reins. 'All right,' she said. 'We're on our way. Hup!'

Orbit moved forward readily and Melanie turned him to

the right, heading for the space between the couch and the wall. There was no more sound from the floor, but with Orbit's first step she felt a faint trembling beneath her feet as the framework of the house adjusted itself to the moving weight. He felt it too. From the corner of her eye she saw his ears snap back in a sign of displeasure. This was something he definitely did not like.

Tightening her grip on the reins, Melanie kept going. There was nothing else to do. From somewhere in the house came a rattle of dishes, and Melanie started talking loudly, saying whatever came into her head.

She passed behind the couch, rounded the corner, and passed the archway to the dining-room. Katie's head appeared to be turning all the way round, like an owl's. On the wall beside the archway hung a mirror just above an antique occasional table that had belonged to Melanie's great-grandmother. The table, which ordinarily held a bowl of flowers and a pair of china figurines, was bare now, like every other surface in the room, and because of its bareness looked even more priceless and perishable than usual.

Probably because Melanie was already thinking ahead, considering what the next move would be, she made the second right turn without taking full account of the width of Orbit's hindquarters. As he came round to pass in front of the couch his left hind leg gently brushed against the little table and it tipped to the right. Her eye caught sight of it a split second too late. It was going to crash to the floor. The crash would startle Orbit. . . . She halted him instantly, her eyes riveted to the teetering antique in a kind of helpless horror.

Farther tipped the table. Farther still . . . then it paused and began to tip back the way it had come. Once its legs hit the floor it toppled the other way, then back and forth until it jiggled itself at last to its original motionless state. Melanie let her breath escape in an enormous sigh, and Katie said in a low, expressionless tone, 'Mellie, how do I look with grey hair?'

Melanie laughed and was startled to find that the laughter

came easily. For no very sound reason the tension was suddenly gone and she felt as completely relaxed as if she had Orbit in the middle of the pasture rather than in the middle of the living-room. What had she been so afraid of anyway? After all, she was Melanie and Orbit was Orbit, and she could handle him every bit as well in one place as another. Just to prove it, she hugged him hard, turned him round in a small, tight circle and walked him round the couch in the opposite direction, bringing him to a halt again with his head towards the dining-room.

Katie, who had lain down again, cradling her head on her folded arms while she watched the performance, said, 'Now that I've got used to the idea, I sort of *like* it. A horse gives a certain *chic* to a house, don't you think?' Changing her voice to an overripe contralto that was supposed to sound like a society lady's, she went on, 'I took tea with Mrs Webb today – Mrs Webb the aah-tist, donchu know? And I met the most chaahm-ing *horse*. He was telling me – '

'Hey!' Melanie interrupted. 'You're supposed to be the hostess around here. The guest is hungry.'

Katie rolled off the couch, landing on her feet. 'Coming right up!' she said, and went out to the kitchen. Returning with the dishpan, she set it in the middle of the dining-table, pulled up a chair for herself and sat down.

Melanie hupped Orbit again and he started up, this time with his ears slanting eagerly forward, all thought of shaky doors and other trivial matters erased from his mind by the lovely raw-vegetable fragrances coming from the dishpan. Halting him with his nose above the table and his tail still in the living-room, Melanie dropped the reins and stood back a step, watching.

After a moment of this Katie asked, 'What are you doing – waiting for him to ask for a fork?'

Melanie shook her head, then half turned, pretending not to watch him. He stood for at least a full minute without moving anything but his eyes and nostrils.

'I get it,' Katie said. 'Discipline.' She paused, then added protestingly, 'Gads, Mellie! The poor beast is dying of *temptation.*'

About to relent, Melanie suddenly saw him begin to reach out his nose – slowly, cautiously. Still pretending not to notice, she let him reach almost to the pan. 'Aaaaaaa*aah*!' The exclamation was a combination of warning, reproval and scorn, and Orbit's head snapped violently back to its proper position, the bridle jangling sharply. He managed to look guilty. '*You* know better than that,' Melanie told him reprovingly. 'You're in the house, and you've got to watch your manners! You didn't really think you'd get away with that did you? Did you really think it would *work*?' The bridle jangled again and the trailing reins whipped in all directions as Orbit shook his head.

'All *right,* then.' She let him wait a few moments longer, then reached up, unbuckled the bridle and slipped it off his head, holding it while he pushed the bit out with his tongue. Then she slapped his neck and he lost no time in helping himself to this unscheduled meal. Chewing loudly and placidly away at his first delicious mouthful, he raised his head and peered down at Katie with a sort of benevolent expression. Propping her chin in the heel of one hand, Katie peered back at him. 'It's funny,' she said, 'but he makes me feel right at home, as if I ought to be passing the biscuits or something.'

Katie had prepared an even more generous serving than her instructions called for, and soon Melanie got tired of standing. Pulling up another chair, she too sat down across from her sister and beside Orbit, resting both elbows on the table.

For a long time neither of them said anything. They merely sat, staring up at Orbit in a kind of trance induced by the leisurely rhythm of his crunching. After a while Melanie dropped her eyes and quite by accident encountered Katie's. They stared at each other, a little blankly at first, then Katie giggled. So did Melanie. A moment later the sound of Orbit's chewing was drowned out by their whoops and shrieks of laughter.

Orbit's ears twitched back, then forward again. His jaws stopped moving, he turned his head towards Melanie and peered at her, his big eyes looking mildly astonished and not altogether approving. This sent Katie into a new spasm of mirth, in which Melanie promptly joined her. They both tried to speak, and both failed utterly.

In the living-room Orbit switched his sweeping tail. In the dining-room he resumed his interrupted meal. In front of the house, the heavy-shouldered stranger who stood with his head beneath the upraised hood of his old car, tinkering with its motor, listened intently to the outburst of laughter. Then he turned and spat with satisfaction into the dust at the side of the road. After days of difficult spying work – of seeing and hearing things without being noticed – everything, apparently, was going along to his satisfaction.

Chapter 11

SOBERING at last, Katie wiped her eyes with her chorus-girl apron and said, 'Do me a favour. Since I'm the official hostess, let me call what's-his-name, the budding journalist, and invite him to the party tomorrow.'

'I don't mind.' Melanie peered more closely at her sister, who was beginning to look fiendish. 'But I'll bet Conrad will.' She stood up. 'Don't do it till I put Orbit out in the pasture. I want to listen.'

Coming back a few minutes later, she leaned in the kitchen doorway while Katie, half sitting on the edge of the telephone table, got Conrad Wemmer on the phone.

'This is Kathleen Webb,' she said. 'Melanie's sister. I'm calling to – Webb. W as in watermelon, E as in elementary, B as in brittlebrain, B as in. . . . What? *Brittlebrain.* I know it isn't; I just made it up. . . . Melanie. Mel-lan-nee. The girl with the horse. . . . Gooooood lad! I knew you'd make it! Want to rest a little before we go on? Okay. I'm calling for Melanie – to invite you to a horse-warming. Tomorrow at. . . . *Horse*-warming. Horse as in steeplechase. No, *steeplechase.* S as in – oh, forget it! Look, Conrad, is your mommie there?'

In the doorway Melanie nearly choked.

'Just 'aving me bit o' fun, dearie,' Katie went on. 'To make it real clear – Mellie wants you to come over tomorrow after-noon so she can prove she keeps her horse in the house. About three o'clock, okay? Wait a minute.' She looked at Melanie. 'He wants to know if he can bring his camera.'

Melanie shook her head violently. 'No! It's got one of those flash things on it. Orbit might jump through the ceiling.'

Katie put the phone to her mouth again. 'Sorry, Conrad, no cameras. Military security, you know. Just bring your beady little eyes. Right. Three o'clock. 'Bye.' She hung up and turned to Melanie. 'You know, with a little study, that boy could learn to be a moron.'

Conrad Wemmer arrived promptly at three the next afternoon, wearing a sceptical grin and a bulky old sweater that looked very strange on a warm June day.

Katie met him at the door, Melanie having decided to go up and change her jeans for jodhpurs. 'Hi, Mr Lippmann,' she greeted him, and eyed the sweater admiringly. 'Taking the moths out for a walk?'

Conrad's ears turned pink. 'Got a cold,' he said, coughing piteously. 'Bad cold.'

'Cold?' said Katie. 'What are you doing for it? I mean, besides wearing that sweater?'

'Doing? Well, I'm – uh – '

'Here.' Katie thrust into his hand half of a potato she had been cutting up for Orbit's snack. 'Eat it,' she commanded. 'It's loaded with vitamins. Best thing in the world for a cold.'

He took the potato, watching Katie warily. Finally he took a bite, apparently deciding that the only safe thing was to humour this large, insane girl.

Katie nodded approvingly. 'When your hostess – which is me – offers you something to eat,' she observed, 'it isn't polite just to *hold* it.'

Conrad was crunching manfully when Melanie clattered down the stairs to his rescue. 'Hi,' she said, then to Katie. 'Everything ready?'

'Soon as I peel one more potato,' Katie said, turning an accusing gaze on her unhappy guest. 'I *did* have enough, but *he's eating* one.'

Thoroughly demoralized, Conrad started to say something, but Melanie, all business, hustled him out into the front yard. 'You wait here while I go and get Orbit. I want him to meet you before we go in.'

Conrad's grin looked a little sickly. 'M-meet me?' As he

spoke he gave an involuntary start, then instantly clamped both arms over his stomach.

Fortunately for him, Melanie wasn't looking at him, having bent down to wedge the door open. Had she been looking she might have discovered one or both of two things Conrad was concealing. Inside his head lay hidden an unreasoning but deathly fear of horses, and inside the folds of his sweater snuggled Conrad's pride and joy – his little candid camera, flashgun attached and ready.

'Sure,' Melanie said, straightening up from the door wedge. 'So he'll be used to having you around.'

When she came back leading Orbit, Conrad was leaning in the doorway with an elaborate air of nonchalance. He seemed to shrink a little as she came closer; and though he spoke to Melanie, his eyes were fastened on Orbit, whose head loomed up over her shoulder. 'Uh, Mellie,' he said. 'Let's just skip the – uh – introduction, and go on in and, well, I'm sort of in a hurry.'

'Oh, it'll only take a second,' Melanie said impatiently. 'Just pet him a little and let him smell you.'

Conrad didn't move. 'I – uh – '

This time Melanie gave him a piercing look. 'Conrad! What's the *matter* with you?'

With the courage of desperation Conrad took a step forward. 'Nothing's the matter.' He stretched out a hand and gave Orbit a gingerly stroke on the tip of the nose. It tickled, Orbit shook his head, and Conrad snatched his hand back as if it had been burned.

Not until then did Melanie understand and feel embarrassed for him. She had known others afraid of horses; and while she would never understand them, she realized vaguely that they couldn't help themselves.

'Well,' she said, trying to sound businesslike instead of embarrassed, 'all you have to do is go in and sit on the couch and watch. Okay?'

'Okay,' said Conrad, relieved but miserable all the same.

Melanie dropped the reins and followed him in. In the living-room he stopped so abruptly that she almost ran into him. There was Katie leaping up and down in front of the couch with as much violence as if she had been on a trampoline instead of a floor. When she saw them she stopped, breathing hard and smiling happily at the two of them. 'There! This floor has now been anaesthetized. Bring on your horse!'

Conrad, looking a little anaesthetized himself, sat where he was told, while Katie perched on an arm of the couch and Melanie went out to get Orbit.

Everything went beautifully. Orbit, who had long since smelled fresh raw vegetables and knew that the better he behaved the sooner he would be juicily crunching them be-tween his teeth, responded to every signal or command the instant it was given. He picked up his feet with dainty cauti-ousness. He hupped, ho'ed, side-stepped, and even backed without once letting his ears show a sign of displeasure. Mel-anie was so full of love and pride and triumph that she actually felt kindly towards Conrad and resolved to top the whole per-formance off with a neat little unrehearsed touch.

Halting Orbit smartly with his head just inside the dining-room archway, she told Katie grandly. 'You may serve dinner now, Kathleen. Conrad, do sit down at the table. I'll just go and wash my hands, and then we'll have dinner.'

She watched while Conrad sidled through the archway and took a chair at the table. Katie brought the dish-pan and sat down, too. In the process she suddenly gave Conrad an odd, wary look which Melanie missed because she was busy drop-ping the reins and stepping back to catch Orbit's eye with a stern glance. 'Stand!' she commanded, then quickly crossed the living-room to the hall and stepped into the bathroom, where she ran water into the bowl just long enough for Conrad to hear it.

Conrad, however, wasn't listening. Emboldened by Orbit's faultless performance, and fortified by his idea of how a keen-eyed news hawk acts, he fumbled inside his baggy sweater, snatched out the little camera, and sighted it straight at Orbit.

Katie stiffened, her eyes widened, and she opened her mouth to cry out. The camera made a tiny crackly snap, the flash flared blindingly, and the faultless performance came to a shattering, explosive end.

Melanie stepped into the room at precisely the right moment to be blinded for a fraction of a second. But she needed no sight to hear the sudden rattle of Orbit's bridle and an instant later, sickeningly, the thud of his head as it struck the archway above it.

'Ho, boy!' The command burst out of her mouth instinctively controlled, neither too loud nor too soft. And with the words she moved, crossing the room swiftly, hand reaching for the bridle. 'Easy now!' she said.

In a moment she would have it and she would be in control of him before the shock of the blow to his head could bring real panic.

The moment never came, because Conrad seized it to go into a panic of his own. The sight of this hitherto mild beast suddenly throwing his great head upwards with eyes rolling fearsomely, and slamming it against the archway, and the guilty knowledge that he himself was to blame, brought Conrad surging to his feet, looking every bit as wild as Orbit. The movement sent his chair crashing against the wall behind him, and Orbit, startled again by this new burst of noise and motion, started to whirl, his hindquarters skittering to the left.

Because he moved, Melanie's reaching hand missed the bridle, reached again, and seized it the instant his left haunch struck the little antique table and slammed it to the floor with a horrible splintering sound. Within the wink of an eye Melanie had thrown her right arm round his neck while yanking downward on the reins with her left, and soothing words were streaming with mechanical calmness from her mouth.

In a matter of seconds she felt him grow calm. Turning,

she met the horrified eyes of Katie, who was still sitting frozen at the table. They stared at each other in bleak silence, then Katie said in a croaking half whisper, 'Get him out of here, Mellie! Oh, golly, get him out of here!'

'He's all right now,' Melanie answered woodenly and her eyes moved beyond Katie to the overturned chair.

'If you're looking for that – that *unspeakable* boy,' Katie said in a stronger voice, 'he's gone. He streaked out through

the kitchen like a – like a scared little rabbit and I hope I never see him again. Mellie, *please* get Orbit out before something else happens.'

Melanie did take him out, but not until he had eaten his treat from the dish-pan on the table. He had earned it with his impeccable behaviour, she felt, and the awful thing that happened was certainly not his fault. It was Conrad's fault, of course, but at bottom it was her own. If only she hadn't left his side for that final stunt!

When she got back to the house, Katie was on her knees beside the little antique, trying hopelessly to hold it up as she slipped one of its shattered legs into place beneath it. Melanie dropped down beside her, staring mutely at the table. The table sagged and wavered in Katie's uncertain grasp – a shapeless, pitiful thing with great white cracks in its time-polished wood.

Melanie felt sicker the more she looked. If only something else – anything else in the house – had been broken! But this table . . . Mom held it in a special sort of affection because it had once been thought beautiful by her mother, who was dead now, and by her mother's mother before that. And now it lay shattered beyond repair, beautiful to nobody at all.

'Well, somebody's got to say something,' Katie said, trying for the light touch and failing miserably. 'But there just isn't anything to say, is there?'

For a moment Melanie was too close to tears to say anything at all. Then she shook her head and managed to blurt out in a voice that sounded more like Pop's than her own, 'Oh, *blast* Conrad Wemmer!'

'That's a step in the right direction,' Katie said, managing a wry smile. '*Double* blast Conrad Wemmer!'

'But it was *my* fault, Katie! Oh, why did I ever – '

'Don't be silly, Mellie. How could you possibly have known the little monster would go popping cameras around? How could you know he'd go into a foaming tizzy the moment Orbit – '

'But I *left* Orbit! I went clear out of the room when I – ' Tears were threatening again, tears of humiliation this time; and the rest of her words came out in a strangled, anguished rush. 'It all happened because I was – was showing off! And, Katie, there's nothing worse around horses than a stupid showoff!'

Katie raised her voice to be heard above the outpouring of self-condemnation; Melanie in turn raised hers; and between them they quite drowned the sound of a car as it turned into the drive. Drowned also were the sounds of footsteps on the path and a twice-repeated knock at the door. The first thing they did hear, when they both had to pause for breath at last, was a man's apologetic cough. They both stiffened and whirled round as well as two girls can whirl, kneeling on a carpeted floor. Simultaneously they cried out, 'Mr Bristow!' and scrambled to their feet.

The tall man's homely face crinkled into its surprising smile and he inclined his head in a miniature bow, half courtly and half humorous. 'I knocked,' he said. 'But the damsel-in-distress noises were too much for me. And now – ' His eyes came to rest on the shattered table. 'And now I think I see what caused them.'

Katie, who could almost always rise to an occasion, rose now. Following his glance, she said solemnly, 'Poor thing. We just couldn't break it of chasing cars.'

He laughed and tilted quizzical eyebrows at Melanie. 'And you couldn't break your horse of romping around in the house?'

They both stared at him, and Melanie said, 'How – how did you know?'

'Sleuth at work,' Mr Bristow said, nodding towards the carpet. 'Hoofprints.' He raised his nose and made sniffing noises. 'Slight odour of horse.' Including both girls in another smile, he added, 'if it's a secret I'm blind, deaf, dumb, and forgetful. So just pretend I – '

'Secret!' Katie burst out. 'Wait and see what a secret it's going to be when *Mom* comes home! Oh, golly, Mr Bristow, we're in the soup up to our pincurls.'

'And it's all my fault!' Melanie chimed in. 'I did the stupidest thing I've done in my whole – '

'For goodness' sake, Mellie, don't start *that* again. It wasn't your fault and you – '

Mr Bristow clasped both hands to his ears and waggled his head from side to side. 'Please, girls, one at a time! Or better still, none at a time, because I'll bet I'm way ahead of you. And the point now – ' He stepped past them and jackknifed himself to a crouch in front of the table. 'The point now is: what are we going to do about it?'

'We?' said Melanie faintly but hopefully.

'Do about it?' repeated Katie. 'Mr Bristow, there's *nothing* we can do about it. It didn't just come apart at the seams. The wood itself is all splintered and cracked. *Look* at it.'

'He *is* looking at it,' Melanie said impatiently.

Because Mr Bristow said nothing else for a moment, they both fell silent, watching his long fingers delicately probe the cracks in the wood. At last he rose, brushing his knees. 'It's bad,' he said. 'But it's not hopeless, and if there's any man in the world who can fix it, I know the man. And he's right in Portland – an old German who used to do work for my father now and then. He can do things with wood that are, well, impossible. So – ' He swung round and strode to the front door, where he called out, 'Will! Step in here for a minute, will you?'

Melanie and Katie stared at each other. Then Melanie remembered. 'He's the young guy who drives Mr Bristow around and – and everything.'

Mr Bristow, returning, overheard this vague explanation and smiled. 'Will's my good right hand,' he said. 'And my memory. Even my conscience sometimes. He's out of college but still studying, and he has the odd idea he can learn something from me. So he does all my dirty work for starvation wages, and we're both happy. Oh, Will, you deserve a treat, so make your bow to the Webb girls. Kathleen, Melanie, Will Dunnaway.'

Melanie realized that the young man, whom she hadn't really looked at when she had run into him down at the river, had humorous eyes behind his heavy-rimmed glasses and a very nice smile. He was taller than she remembered, too, and in spite of the glasses and his dark, rather formal looking business suit he somehow had the look of an athlete. She was in the middle of deciding she liked him very much when she caught sight of Katie's face.

Katie was looking at him with as much intense, expectant interest as if he had just arrived bearing gifts from a hitherto little-known planet.

She turned what Melanie thought was a very attractive rose colour.

Mr Bristow turned to Will. 'At the moment, Will, we've got a first-aid operation on our hands.' He nodded towards the table. 'Lend me a hand. We'll put it in the car and take it to an antique furniture magician.'

The moment the two men went out, carrying their burden cautiously, Katie exploded into activity. 'Mellie, come on!' she said urgently, seizing one end of the big couch, which still stood in the middle of the room. 'This place looks like a – a *bus* station! No, wait, I'll move this. You get that awful dish-pan off the dining-table and clean up Orbit's droolings. And get out the lamps and ashtrays and all that stuff you put in the cupboard. Hurry! And I'll go start some coffee. Men always want coffee. And there's some cake left. And – oh *blast*! Why did I have to put on these *mildewed* old shorts!'

Melanie, who was hurrying as fast as she could to obey even one of the machine-gunned commands, slowed suddenly, feeling curiously rigid. Mr Bristow! Orbit! In all the excitement, she had forgotten. But here he was, and apparently in no great hurry this time. With any ingenuity at all she could get him aside. It was up to her to do it. Any minute now. With unsteady hands she began mechanically to clean up after Orbit.

In all the confusion, the chance didn't come immediately. Katie persuaded the visitors to settle down with coffee and cake, and as they did so Melanie was struck by another thought. 'Oh golly,' she burst out, 'we were so wrapped up in ourselves we didn't even ask what. . . . You came to see Pop, didn't you? And he won't be home till Monday!'

Mr Bristow nodded, smiling. 'I did, but this is so nice I'm not even sorry I missed him.' He went on to explain that he had appointments in British Columbia the next day, that the whole trip had come up unexpectedly and that he had decided on the spur of the moment to make part of the trip on the river in his boat perhaps to catch Pop at home in the process.

'But it doesn't matter,' he said. 'If your father's going to be back the first of the week I'll see him then – unless, of course, something else comes up meanwhile.' He threw Will an ironic glance. 'Poor Will. He has a terrible time keeping track of my travel arrangements – always having to shuttle me from cars to boats to trains to aeroplanes.'

'Not to mention snowsleds,' Will put in. 'And mule carts.'

'Well, that doesn't happen often.' Mr Bristow thought for a moment. 'Let's see, Will, I'll fly to Vancouver tonight, so you'll be stuck with the car and the boat, so – '

He and his Good Right Arm went on to make a lot of complicated arrangements, which included leaving the boat keys with Katie and Melanie until either Mr Bristow or Will came back to get the boat, depending on whatever might be decided about the car and the boat in the meantime. Melanie quickly lost track, while Katie, she could tell, was paying no attention at all. When Mr Bristow looked at his watch with an exclamation, she couldn't suppress a look of disappointment and an exclamation of her own. '*Don't* say you have to go! There's gallons of coffee!'

Mr Bristow was already on his feet, but Melanie saw by the way his eyes moved from Katie to Will and back again that he hadn't missed the flash of disappointment. 'Afraid we'll have to get to the hotel. Phone calls and all that. But wait! Just had an idea. Why don't you girls do Will and me the honour of having dinner with us tonight? We'll have a night on the town – dining, dancing, the works! Will can fetch you. You can all wave me a sad farewell at the airport, and then he'll drive you home.'

Melanie looked at Katie, Katie looked at Melanie, and Mr Bristow said, 'Then it's all settled. I won't take no for an answer.'

Nobody, it seemed, had any intention of giving him no for an answer. Melanie welcomed the invitation because it meant she could put off her talk with Mr Bristow for at least a few hours. A minute later he and his Right Arm had driven off, leaving the girls in something of a daze on the front step.

Katie broke the silence with a deep sigh.

Melanie said a little uneasily, 'What do you wear to a night on the town? And have we got any?'

The answer – there really wasn't any choice – was the dresses for Diane's graduation, and they were a great success. So was the night on the town. At the hotel dining-room they feasted at Mr Bristow's suggestion on things with long French names and long American prices. After that they went to a French movie which Melanie found very funny even though she had to depend on the English sub-titles to tell her what was being said. Katie, on the other hand, had studied French for three years and Melanie was quite snobbishly proud of her because she always laughed right along with Will and Mr Bristow, without having to wait for the sub-titles.

After that they went dancing – or rather Katie and Will went dancing while Mr Bristow and Melanie sat at a little table, sipping delicious tall drinks and talking. Actually, Mr Bristow was the only one who could be said to be talking. Melanie's contributions consisted mostly in swallowing hard and replying rather disjointedly to his remarks. She was trying to get up her nerve.

Perhaps she would never have done it if Mr Bristow had not said, with his sympathetic smile, 'all right, Melanie, what is it? Why not say it and get it over with?'

She smiled fleetingly, feeling sheepish as well as nervous. Then she swallowed harder than ever and blurted in a voice that sounded thin and reedy in her ears, 'Would you – would you still want . . . to buy Orbit?'

There was a long stillness during which a man's voice rumbled something at a near-by table and a woman laughed screechily. Melanie's chest felt painfully tight and full, as if she were having the flu again. Then he said quietly, 'Of course I would. Is he for sale?'

She nodded. For the life of her she could do nothing else, and she wished he would stop looking at her with those uncomfortably penetrating eyes.

At that instant he did shift his gaze, looking down at his glass. She had to tell herself that of course he hadn't read the thought in her eyes. Then he said calmly, 'Well now, let's see. I'll buy him all right – give you a cheque tonight if you like. But I won't have any place to keep him until my house is built. Could you keep him for me until then?'

'Oh, yes!' The words leaped out before she saw that his eyes were probing into hers again. If he saw how eager she was he'd know she didn't really want to sell Orbit and perhaps wouldn't buy him. 'I mean,' she amended hastily, 'I mean I could arrange to do that.'

'I'll pay his board, of course.'

'Oh, no!' The thought of taking money for the privilege of keeping Orbit seemed terribly wrong. But again she wished she hadn't been so vehement. Somehow or other she had again betrayed herself, and again she floundered. 'You don't need to do that. I've got plenty of hay and – and everything.'

He shook his head, looking firm. 'No, I'll pay you. We're friends, but that's all the more reason for keeping this strictly a business deal.' He leaned forward, putting his elbows on the table. 'Now we come to the matter of price. Since this is a business deal, let me remind you that it's the seller's job to sell dear and the buyer's job to buy cheap. And I warn you, I'm known to drive a hard bargain. So it's your move. What are you asking?'

Melanie was suddenly struck dumb. In all her frantic struggling and thinking and decision making she had never once thought of a price. Such a situation as this – sitting down and bargaining – had not for an instant occurred to her. Finding her voice at last, she said desperately, 'C-couldn't you just tell me how much you'd – '

He was shaking his head. 'Bargaining begins with the asking price. You name it.'

Her mind raced. To her, Orbit was worth a million dollars, or any other inconceivable sum. But now she had to be practical. She had to think of a sum that somebody would actually pay. But what sum? Suddenly, a figure leaped into her mind from nowhere. No, not from nowhere, but from her talk with Katie. It was the sum that represented four years of college. Before she could lose her nerve, she blurted it out. 'Ten thousand dollars!'

She watched his face anxiously, looking for a clue to his reaction. For a moment she thought she saw a gleam of something in his eyes. Could it be amusement? But no, it couldn't be, because after thinking a little he said slowly, 'Well now, that's just a little steep. What do you say to five thousand? After all, there are a lot of mighty fine horses I could buy for less than – '

'Well, they wouldn't be Orbit!' she interrupted hotly, completely forgetting her uncertainty in her outrage at the thought of comparing Orbit with other horses.

'That's true, all right,' Mr Bristow said grudgingly, 'but five thousand dollars is a lot of money.'

'Well, it's not enough,' Melanie said recklessly. She had never seen even as much as a hundred dollars at one time, but now five thousand seemed a paltry amount. 'Ten thousand dollars!' she repeated, wishing she had made it twenty.

He toyed with his glass and sighed with resignation. 'I'll go to seventy-five hundred, but that's my limit.'

Melanie, who wasn't aware that her eyes were sparkling with excitement nor that she was losing contact with reality, spoke promptly. 'Ten thousand!'

For the second time she saw that gleam in his eyes, and this time he did smile, though ruefully. 'I'm supposed to be the hard-bargain man around here. All right, I'll go to eight-five hundred. Not a nickel more.'

'Oh,' said Melanie faintly.

'Is it a deal?' asked Mr Bristow.

At that moment the band made a little curlicue of sound and stopped. Melanie looked up to see people leaving the dance floor, among them Katie and Will. 'Yes,' she said quickly, 'it's a – a deal. And, Mr Bristow, *please* don't say anything to Katie.'

'Not a word,' he said promptly.

Katie and Will scarcely paused for the ordinary pleasantries, picking up an animated conversation which had been going on while they had danced. It was about something called existentialism, and Will looked amazed that Katie should know as much about it as she did.

They kept it up until the band started, then got up, still talking, and went out on the dance floor again. Melanie watched them go with a lift of happiness. Katie looked really pretty tonight, because she was so happy. And with Will she didn't look big at all, because he was so much bigger.

Mr Bristow's voice startled her by echoing her thoughts. 'She's really a remarkable girl.'

'Oh, she *is*!' Melanie turned a glowing face towards him. 'You wouldn't believe how clever she is!' Because of the music, the grand surroundings, the whole exciting evening, she allowed herself to be carried away. 'She's going to go to college back east – to Columbia! Even if Diane can't go where she wants to, Katie *can*, and it's really much more important for Katie because she's such a brilliant student. Mr Emerson – he's the high school principal – told Mom there was just no limit to what Katie could –'

She stopped, struck by the strange, unreadable expression on his face. Then he smiled. 'She's a brilliant girl,' he said, nodding slightly, 'and a very, very lucky one.'

She stared at him, puzzled.

'Lucky to be brilliant,' he added quickly. Once more the music came to an end and Mr Bristow turned businesslike again. 'Shall I mail you a cheque?'

For the second time Melanie was cast adrift on an uncharted sea. What in the world did a person do with eighty-five hundred dollars which nobody was supposed to know she had? 'Well, couldn't you,' she floundered, 'just wait until — until I have to have it?'

He thought a moment. 'I'll tell you what. I'll put it in a savings account in your name and mail you the pass-book. You won't need to tell anybody about it until you're ready. How will that do?'

She muttered that it would do very well and was mercifully spared the necessity for saying anything else by the return of Katie and Will.

It was midnight when Will unlocked the front door and went into the dark house ahead of them. 'Burglar check,' he explained. The girls turned lights on for him while he walked through the rooms.

'What would you do if you found one?' Melanie asked, mainly to make conversation, because Katie seemed to have become unusually silent.

'Steal everything he's got,' Will answered.

When she had gone, Katie kicked off her shoes and flopped on Pop's big couch, smiling at Melanie and looking rather starry-eyed. 'Trouble with being Cinderella,' she observed, wiggling her toes, 'is that sooner or later the golden coach turns back into a pumpkin.'

'Well,' Melanie said, kicking off her own shoes, 'don't forget what happened to Cinderella in the end.' She went to the back hall and slipped into her old boots.

When Katie saw her she stopped looking wistful long enough to grin at the combination of party dress and battered old boots. 'Now there's a fetching outfit,' she said. 'Latest ensemble for grooming horses in the middle of the night.'

'I'm not going to groom him,' Melanie said. 'Just going to say good night.'

When she got to the barn, though, she didn't say good night. There was nobody to say good night to. Orbit was gone.

Chapter 12

IT seemed to Melanie later that she knew, even before she flipped the switch to flood the stable with light, that Orbit was not in his stall, nor in the corral or pasture beyond. It was as if a chill of awareness had swept over her.

The merest glance showed that the stall was empty, and an instant later her eyes were fixed, as they were meant to be, on the only object in the room that had no business being where it was. Fastened in obvious haste by a single nail to the box stall's corner post was a scrap of board about a foot long. On the face of it were scratches made by something sharp, like the point of a nail. A message!

Her heart pounding high in her throat, Melanie stepped quickly to the board and read the message hastily printed in capital letters:

TRAILING HORSETHIEF NO TIME EXPLAIN STAY BY FONE
RITCH

Melanie read the message, stared wildly around, read it again, then dashed to the door and peered blindly into the dark pasture, knowing it was a pointless thing to do. Thoughts rushed into her mind, like winds, and out again. For a moment they threatened to turn into a waking nightmare and she felt almost sick with the effort of controlling herself. This time there was no Pop to slap her out of a fit of hysterics. Pop was somewhere between San Francisco and home, and there was no way to reach him. Orbit was gone, stolen by the mysterious stranger – and once more, as in the horrible case of Gigi, everything was Melanie's own fault. She hadn't told Pop. She hadn't even told Katie . . .

A second later she was running full tilt for the house, and as she did so she became vaguely aware that it had begun to rain.

At the kitchen table Katie was eating a piece of cake. Her face wore a dreamy look which vanished the instant Melanie burst through the door, her eyes filled with tears.

Katie let Melanie's first storm of words break over her, then got up and, with both hands on her sister's shoulders, forced her into a chair. Raising her voice every time Melanie threatened to burst into speech again, she said, 'Mellie honey, you're not *making any sense* at all, and unless you make sense

there's no *way I can help you*, is there? So just start all over and tell me one *thing at a time*. Slowly. Okay?'

Furiously blinking back the tears, Melanie nodded and began in a strangled voice that soon grew almost normal. Katie merely nodded now and then to show that she understood.

Coming at last to a faltering halt, Melanie stared hopelessly at her sister, who stood by the table deep in thought. 'If only,' Katie said slowly, 'Ritchie had given some idea of what *time* it was when he wrote the message. . . .' She went on, thinking aloud: 'It could have been any time after we left home, and that was five-thirty. But it was *probably* after dark, because people don't usually steal things in broad daylight, and it gets dark after nine, so . . .'

Melanie wasn't even listening, and she couldn't keep still any longer. 'How could they do it?' she burst out. 'How? Katie, he won't go with anybody! Especially a stranger. He'd do something awful to them – I know he would! He . . .'

'He'd go with them,' Katie said slowly, 'if he'd been doped.'

'Doped?'

'Tranquillizing drugs, Mellie. And don't look so wild; they don't harm an animal. Zoos use them to calm animals down so they can treat them when they're sick.'

'Not Orbit!' Melanie objected violently. 'He won't even let Doc Bradley get near him unless I'm there.'

Katie shook her head inexorably. 'You have just told me that this man got close enough to feed Orbit oats. Twice. Oats in one hand, a needle in the other – simple.'

Melanie heard the words in stricken silence, unconsciously holding her folded arms tight against herself like a person trying to keep warm. In a hopeless, desolate tone she said, 'Why didn't I tell you – or Pop? Why?'

'Never mind all that!' Katie straightened resolutely and turned towards the hall door. 'We've got to do something, and the only thing I can think of that's at all practical is to call the highway patrol.'

Melanie was on her feet in an instant. Why hadn't she thought of this herself? 'Do it right now. Hurry!'

Katie started towards the door, with Melanie close behind, when she stopped suddenly, frowning. 'Did that message say "trailing"? He was *trailing* the horsethief?'

Melanie nodded, watching her sister's face anxiously.

'I wonder what he meant?' Katie said, thinking aloud again. 'If he was going to trail him he must have had some way of doing it. You said the man had a horse trailer, so he must have taken Orbit in that, which means Ritchie would have to . . . Mellie, does Ritchie drive a car?'

'Well, he's only got a learner's licence,' Melanie said impatiently. 'But what does that have to do with . . . ?'

In the hall the telephone burst into jangling sound and both girls jumped, staring wildly at each other. 'Ritchie!' Melanie shrieked, and dashed for the phone.

But it wasn't Ritchie. A deep voice said, 'Is this the J. R. Webb residence?'

'Yes,' Melanie replied, her voice flat with disappointment. 'If you want my father, he's not . . .'

'Is this Miss Melanie Webb?'

This time her voice came out in a whisper. 'Y-yes.'

'This is the Oregon State Police. Officer Murdock speaking.'

Melanie's legs felt suddenly weak. She swallowed convulsively. 'Huh – how do you do!' she said idiotically.

'Miss Webb,' the voice went on, somehow giving her the idea that Officer Murdock was smiling, 'would you mind answering a few questions?'

'N-no.' Melanie threw a wild glance at Katie and managed to gasp out for her benefit the word 'police'.

'Will you tell me, Miss Webb, if you are acquainted with a young man named Penfield – *Ritchie* Penfield?'

'Ritchie! What – ? Where is he? Is he there? How did you – ' The questions came pouring out of Melanie and she couldn't stop them. 'Did you find Orbit? Oh, please, is he all right? Where – ?'

Suddenly Katie's hand closed over her wrist and Melanie found the phone being gently but firmly removed from her grasp. Then Katie was speaking. 'This is Melanie's older sister. Would you mind speaking to me? She's a little upset. . . . Yes, that's right, I'm Kathleen Webb.'

With one foot Katie shoved the telephone table stool towards Melanie and nodded towards it while she talked. Melanie sank down on it obediently.

'Yes,' Katie said into the phone. 'It's Fred. Fred L. Penfield, I think. . . . No, but it must be Route Two, Cascade, because they're on the same mail route as we are.'

Melanie listened dully, her hopeful excitement gone. She knew Orbit hadn't been found. If he had been, the police wouldn't be asking all these silly questions, such as the name and address of Ritchie's father.

There was a long pause, then Katie said, 'That's right, Officer. We didn't discover he was missing until just a little while ago. . . . Yes. . . . No.'

The yesses and noes and pauses went on for a long time. Melanie all but stopped listening. She could think of only one thing – that Orbit had not been found. He was gone – Heaven knew where! – in the hands of strange men who didn't love him, however much they might value him, and she, Melanie Webb, might as well be dead.

She didn't even notice when Katie hung up the phone at last and stood looking down at her, but she couldn't help hearing when Katie suddenly burst out, 'For goodness sake, Mellie, stop sitting there like a lump! Orbit isn't *dead* – and in about five minutes every police officer in the state will be on the lookout for him. And if you're only thinking about how *you* feel, try thinking about how *Ritchie* feels. He's up to his ears in trouble, and all on account of you!'

This outburst of scolding accomplished just what it was supposed to. It brought Melanie to her feet, eyes wide. 'Trouble? What kind of trouble?'

'Trouble with the law!' Katie began making a list on her fingers. 'Theft of a motor vehicle, driving without a licence, exceeding the speed limit, reckless driving – think of anything else and he's probably guilty of that, too!'

'Oh, no!'

'Come on,' Katie commanded, starting for the kitchen. 'I'm going to recruit my strength with some hot chocolate, and so are you. In the process I'll tell you everything I know. What I don't know you'll find out from Ritchie when they bring him here.'

'When who bring him here?' Melanie said ungrammatically.

'The police, silly! He's too young to be thrown in jail, and they can't turn him loose with a car again for fear he might overthrow the government, or something, so they're bringing him here. Now do be quiet and *listen*.'

While Melanie leaned against a kitchen counter and listened with numb obedience, Katie banged pans around, making chocolate, and talking.

'What happened before your knight-errant ran afoul of the law,' she began, 'I can only guess, but I'll bet it's a durn *good* guess. I'll bet he showed up here, riding Baldy, just in time to catch sight of your mystery man as he started off down the road with Orbit in his trailer. Knowing he couldn't follow the man very far on Baldy, he very sensibly hightailed it for home and borrowed his father's car without asking. This took some time, giving Mystery Man a good head start. Then Ritchie wasted more time dashing up and down the back roads around here before deciding that if the man came from Nevada he would likely go back there by the quickest way possible, which would be the Freeway through Salem and Eugene.

'Anyway, Patrolman Murdock entered the picture about an hour ago while he was cruising northbound on the Freeway between Albany and Salem. They told him on the radio to get over in the southbound lanes and intercept some crazy juvenile delinquent who'd been spotted passing the Salem turnoff a few minutes before, going about ninety in what probably was a stolen car.

'Murdock was just getting into position when he saw a horse-trailer go by – Nevada licence – with a horse in it. He – '

'A horse!' Melanie screamed the words. 'Katie was – '

'I said be *quiet*! About three minutes later here came the car he was waiting for. He flipped on his blinker light and started moving. Zoom went Ritchie, and zoom went Murdock, full speed ahead and siren whooping. About a mile farther on, he was closing in on Ritchie when Ritchie's tail lights sort of got all mixed up with another set of tail lights and by the time Murdock came to a screeching halt on the shoulder of the road he saw that Ritchie had cut in front of the car with the horse-trailer, forcing him off on to the shoulder and practically into the ditch. And now there he was, yanking at the door handle of Mystery Man's car and yelling at him to get out and fight like a man.'

Katie raised her voice and talked even faster, obviously aware that Melanie was about to burst out again. 'Murdock ordered Ritchie to cease and desist, or whatever it is, and got him calmed down enough to make some kind of sense. But the only sense he made was to accuse the man flatly of stealing Orbit, and . . .'

This time Melanie would not be shushed. 'Well, he *did* steal him! Orbit was right there in the trailer. Katie, if you don't tell me how he *is* – '

She broke off as Katie shook her head violently. 'Mellie, I'm trying to *tell* you. It wasn't Orbit! The horse in the trailer *was not* Orbit!'

Katie set a steaming cup of chocolate in front of Melanie, who stared at it as if she had never seen such a thing before and had no idea what to do with it. Katie went on. 'It was a palomino mare, and your cowboy friend produced a bill of sale for it. He'd bought it over near Molalla. Hadn't stolen anything at all. So the patrolman let him go. And he's called for another patrolman to drive Ritchie's father's car. They're going to come here, and ask some more questions, I suppose, so there's nothing we can do now but wait. Drink your chocolate.'

Melanie did as she was told, because it was less trouble than trying to explain that she couldn't possibly drink anything at all. When it was finished she allowed Katie to manoeuvre her to a chair in the living-room. One thing was clear – brutally clear. Orbit was gone and there was no very convincing reason to suppose that she would ever see him again.

In the living-room Katie ranged restlessly around, pointlessly tidying things up. And she talked. She said vague, comforting, confident things which neither of them believed.

She was rattling on in this vein when she suddenly interrupted herself with an exclamation and slapped her forehead with genuine disgust. 'Stupid me! Oh, what a dimwit! Mellie, while all this business about the man from Nevada was going on, did you notice anything *else* unusual? Did you ever see him talking to anybody? Did any *other* stranger act interested in Orbit?'

Melanie made a bewildered effort to struggle up out of her mental fog. 'N-no,' she said hoarsely because her throat needed clearing. 'But – but what are you . . .'

Katie gestured impatiently. 'Of course you didn't. Stupid question. The other man would have been very careful not to be seen.'

She paused and Melanie saw her familiar frown of concentration. 'What other man?' Melanie asked, completely baffled.

Katie stopped pacing and stood looking down at her, still frowning. 'Don't you *see*? Your mysterious stranger is a red herring! He was trying to make you suspicious *on purpose*. He wanted you to think just what you did think, and what Ritchie thought, so that somebody would go charging down the highway after him. Mellie, it's his *accomplice* who has Orbit – right this minute! And he's sneaking off in some other direction. By this time he could be half-way to Canada, or Idaho, or *anywhere*.'

She dropped to the couch beside Melanie and seized her by the forearms, fixing her with intense eyes and shaking her a little. '*Think*, Mellie, *think*! Have you noticed any other strangers around? Probably a man, a man who looked as if he's worked with horses a lot. Think *hard*, Mellie!'

Melanie tried. She did her best, relieved that her mind could be put to work at something with a purpose rather than merely exist as a race-track for useless, frantic impressions. While Katie watched anxiously, she searched every corner of her memory for strange faces, for sights, sounds, snatches of conversation, anything the least out of the ordinary. But nothing came – at least nothing useful, nothing she could pin down and look at squarely. At one moment her mind's eye focused fleetingly on a slippery, elusive little fragment of memory. The rest of her mind clutched desperately at it. There was a face connected with it – a not-very-pleasant face, a man's face. There was a wavery impression of light around it. And then it was gone, swallowed up in blackness. Try as she might, scowling fiercely in concentration, she couldn't summon it up again.

She was shaking her head, staring miserably up into her sister's eyes, when both of them heard the faint squeal of tyres on the road as a car swept into the drive.

Chapter 13

FRAMED by the doorway in the yellowish beam of the porch-light, a gentle rain etching the black night behind him with silver, the highway patrolman looked to Melanie like all the world's tall, strong men rolled into one. The sight of him, idiotically, made her want to cry.

His eyes moved from the big girl to the small one and he smiled as he touched the visor of his cap in a half salute. 'Good evening,' he said apologetically. 'I've brought the prisoner. May we come in?'

He stepped aside then, and there was Ritchie Penfield in his silly old baseball shirt, his wiry blond hair bright with raindrops and his generous mouth wide with a sheepish grin. 'I asked him to put me in handcuffs,' Ritchie said as he stepped across the threshold, 'so I could make a real entrance, but he – '

Ritchie got no further. His grin wilted. Melanie had turned away abruptly, thrown her hands to her face, and was weeping helplessly into them.

For once she didn't care. On top of everything else the sight of Ritchie and the knowledge of the terrible trouble he had got himself into on her behalf were simply too much for her, and there was nothing she could do about it except to cry as quietly as possible.

She couldn't see the looks that passed between the other persons in the hall, but she heard Katie's voice, speaking quickly. 'Come in and sit down, Officer.' She heard their steps as they moved into the living-room. Then she felt Ritchie's arm round her shoulders, rough and awkward, and heard his voice, which sounded more panic-stricken than comforting. 'Gee, Mellie, don't! We'll find Orbit. He'll be okay. *Please*, Mellie!'

Then Katie's voice again – wonderful Katie, who seemed always to know just the right thing to do. 'Mellie, be a doll and go brew up a pot of coffee, will you? The lieutenant could use a little something stimulating.'

As Melanie hurried blindly, gratefully, from the room, she heard the patrolman chuckle and say, 'Just what I need, Miss Webb. And thanks for the promotion.'

'Don't even mention it,' Katie said graciously. 'Ritchie, for Heaven's sake sit down and stop looking shell-shocked.'

In the kitchen Melanie combined coffee-making with pulling herself together. At the sink she splashed cold water on her face and dried it fiercely with a towel, taking, in the process, a solemn oath that from now on, whatever happened, she would not disgrace herself again. By the time the percolator had bubbled itself to a standstill she was able to pour out a cup with steady hands and carry it in to the officer with what almost passed for a cheerful smile.

When she brought a second cup for Ritchie, Katie looked at her approvingly and said, 'Mellie, I've been asking questions, in my subtle way, and everything happened almost exactly the way I guessed it did. I was even right in deducing that the man must have turned Orbit over to an accomplice!'

'Wait a minute!' Murdock protested, smilingly shaking his

head. 'I didn't say you were right; I only said the same thing had occurred to me.'

'Sure!' put in Ritchie, leaning forward excitedly. 'But that's the way it *has* to be. After all, I saw the guy steal him, and – '

'No, you didn't.' Murdock drew a little black leather notebook from an inside pocket of his tunic and thumbed through it until he found what he was looking for. 'You saw a 1955 Chevy two-door pulling a loaded single-horse trailer out on to the road from the lane here. You didn't see the driver of the car because it was dark and you were too far away.' He smiled faintly and added, 'Just what you told me.'

'Well, anyway,' Ritchie said, eyeing the notebook as if it had betrayed him, 'it *had* to be him, and if you hadn't let him go . . .'

Katie interrupted firmly. 'Ritchie, I think Officer Murdock knows more about who to arrest and who not to than you do.'

The officer put in, 'Don't worry about our friend from Nevada. We can put our hands on him any time we want to. Meanwhile, if we could get some kind of a line on this other man, if there is one. Any little detail at all . . .'

He looked at Melanie hopefully and she shook her head. 'My sister already asked me to think – and I thought. But – but I just couldn't *get* it.'

There was a brief silence, during which she was conscious that the patrolman was eyeing her thoughtfully. Then he repeated her words. '*Get* it? Then there is something – something you can almost remember, but not quite?'

Meanie hesitated before nodding unhappily. 'I – I *think* so, but . . .'

'Well, never mind,' Murdock said comfortingly, putting his empty cup down. 'It'll probably come back to you, and you can let us know.' He stood up, sliding the notebook back inside his tunic. 'Right now, if you don't mind, I'll take a look round out where you keep the horse. The prisoner here can show me the way.'

137

'I'll go, too!' Melanie said promptly, eager to do anything at all besides just stand around and think.

Murdock smiled a little wryly at her eagerness. 'Don't expect anything. I'm just a cop, not a detective.'

Katie got up too. 'I'll make myself useful,' she said, 'by taking some coffee out to the other officer.'

Melanie stared at her blankly. 'Other officer?'

'I *told* you, Mellie,' Katie said. 'But you weren't listening. It took *two* policemen to bring Ritchie in, one to bring Mr Penfield's car and one to drive the patrol car. Remember?'

Melanie did, but only vaguely. She turned and followed Officer Murdock, who in turn was following Ritchie through the kitchen on the way to the barn.

The unoccupied stable, when Melanie flipped the light switch by the door, was intolerably desolate and empty. The saddles under their canvas covers, the bridles with their polished metalwork glinting in the yellow light, the combs and brushes on their wall pegs, cruelly mocked her with their uselessness. She felt useless herself, like a captain without a ship. Yet somewhere, *somewhere* in this nightmarish world, Orbit existed. All nine-hundred-odd nervous, dangerous pounds of him were somewhere at this very minute jolting along through strange country, more than likely, in some loathsome truck bound for a destination from which he never would return. And here and now, locked in this solid-bone head of hers, was some sly, shifty little detail – she was sure of it now – which held a shred of a clue, a whisper of hope . . .

Unconsciously she shook her head violently and made her eyes focus on Ritchie, who had stepped over to the corner of the stall and yanked loose the board on which he had scribbled his message. As he did so he gave her a side-long look and an apologetic grin. 'Didn't have time to spell everything right,' he said. Picking up the hammer dropped in his haste all those hours ago, he pulled the nail from the board and put it in his pocket with the mechanical caution of country-bred boys who have grown up with livestock in their care.

Officer Murdock, who had been looking around with the concentrated air of a man who is memorizing the scene before him, produced a small flashlight and stepped back outside the barn. Melanie watched him play his beam of light around on the gravelled lane outside the door, bending down for a closer look. After a minute he straightened and said regretfully, 'Too bad it's gravelled. No tracks.' He held the light steady and pointed. 'But it does look as if that line is where the tailgate of the trailer rested. The guy must have loaded the horse right here.' He looked at Melanie. 'Does he load easily?'

She shook her head. 'Only for me. Nobody else can do it. He must have been – ' she hesitated but made herself say the hateful word – 'drugged.'

'Well, it won't do him any harm,' said Murdock, so quickly that she knew he had already thought of this. 'It'll wear off in a few hours.' He looked at his watch. 'Two-fifteen,' he said. 'Let's go, Penfield. Time we got you and your stolen property home.'

In the kitchen, Katie greeted them with a triumphant look. 'Old Auntie Kate has fixed everything up!' she announced, then addressed her remarks to Officer Murdock. 'I just phoned the prisoner's mother. She says if you don't object he can spend the rest of the night here. I'll drive the car home in the morning, and she'll bring me back. You and your colleague won't have to bother about it, so you can rush on back and patrol things.'

Ritchie was staring at her. 'Gee, how did you – '

'Never mind,' Katie told him impatiently, and looked appealingly at the patrolman. 'Since you know all about it, couldn't you just – sort of – *forget* about all those charges, and . . .'

But Murdock was shaking his head regretfully. 'It just doesn't work that way,' he said. 'I've got to write a report on the thing, and, regardless of his good intentions, our young friend here did manage to break a whole bookful of laws in a very short space of time. I'll do what I can, but – ' He shrugged and looked uncomfortable.

Melanie had to suffer a new pang of guilt. Thinking of nothing but Orbit, she had already forgotten that Ritchie, on her account, was in trouble up to his ears.

Officer Murdock started out to the waiting patrol car. The others went with him, conversing politely, as though there were nothing at all unusual about bidding farewell to a guest in a policeman's uniform in the small hours of the morning.

As they approached the wetly gleaming police car, Melanie's ears caught the crackling, staccato sound of its radio. The officer inside was a formless shadow in the rainy dark.

Then abruptly there came a flare of yellowish light. The policeman's face leaped into life as he held a match to his cigarette, and Melanie froze in her tracks.

The others moved on, not noticing she had stopped, and in a moment the face vanished again into blackness. But Melanie stood still, caught in a bewildering, dizzy whirl of tormented thought. But why? What was it? She didn't know, and yet it seemed as if not knowing would quickly drive her out of her mind. It wasn't the face. She knew she had never seen the face before. Then why should she feel almost sick with frustration? It had something to do with that tiny detail that lay maddeningly buried somewhere inside her head. She had to remember it! She *had* to – but she couldn't.

She was conscious of the voices around her as good-byes were said, heard the patrol car's motor purr into throaty life, saw the car back and turn and slide away down the road, its tail-lights winking farewell. Turning with the others, she walked back into the house, saying nothing, feeling as if she were not really there. And all the time she was entreating, cajoling, commanding her untrustworthy brain: Remember! Remember!

She was only vaguely conscious of Ritchie's insisting to Katie that he would sleep in the barn, of Katie's arm firmly propelling her up the stairs, and of her voice: 'You're done in, Mellie, but you're all wound up like a toy train. I'm going to give you one of Mom's sleeping pills. When you wake up they'll have found Orbit and we'll all live happily ever after.'

In the bathroom Melanie tucked the little red pill under her tongue and drank the water Katie thrust at her. After her sister had said good night she took the pill out and dropped it into her waste-basket. She couldn't have told anyone why she did it. She had no plan that could possibly be served by wakefulness. There was no motive at all beyond a pointless, stubborn determination to stay awake until something happened – or until she dropped.

With wooden, automatic movements she undressed, switched off the light, and lay staring steadily into the darkness. Oddly, the longer she lay there the calmer she became, and the more stubborn. Over and over she kept telling herself there was a way out of this. There had to be. And it was up to her to think of it.

It was something about a flare of light. Something about a man lighting a match. Man lighting cigarette. Cigar. Pipe. Man cupping hands round match to light pipe. PIPE!

In a flash she was on her feet, fumbling with one shaky hand for the lamp switch, and groping for her jeans with the other.

A minute later she was flipping the light on in the stable and mercilessly shaking the bulky form that lay wrapped, head and all, in a cocoon of blanket.

'Get up, Ritchie! Get up!' she commanded. 'Get up. I know where Orbit is! They've taken him up the river in a house-boat!'

Chapter 14

THERE was a writing upheaval on the bunk and Ritchie's face appeared, eyes startled and uncomprehending. 'Whuh – huh – whussmatter?' he said.

'Wake *up*, Ritchie!' Melanie said with passionate impatience. 'I *remembered*! And you've got to help me. Hurry!'

The fog of sleep swept away, his eyes focused and he sat up, pushing the blanket aside. 'Okay,' he said, keeping his eyes on her while his feet worked their way into his shoes. 'What are we going to do?'

The words tumbled out of Melanie. 'I *remembered*, Ritchie! I don't know how, but I did. It was a man – sort of rough-looking with a seamy face and dirty grey hair. I saw him one night down at the boat landing, inside a big, ugly houseboat. I didn't pay much attention, but something stuck in my mind and I didn't know what it was until now. He lit a pipe, and he did it to try to hide his face because he saw me looking at him. He's the other man! The accomplice! And they planned all along to hide Orbit inside and take him up the river because nobody would ever think to look for a horse in a houseboat!'

Ritchie started to say something, but she plunged ahead. 'And somewhere up the river – miles from here – they'll go ashore and transfer him to a truck or something, if they haven't done it already by now.' Her voice rose. 'So we've got to *hurry*, Ritchie. We've got to –'

'Hurry and do *what*, Mellie?' he said, getting a word in at last.

'Go after him, of course,' she said impatiently. She whirled and stepped over to the wall where her riding tack hung on its row of neatly spaced pegs.

'But how?' Ritchie demanded, getting to his feet and staring at the back of her head with troubled eyes. 'We can't *swim* up the river!'

Melanie paused, eyeing the bridles consideringly. Strangely, she was beginning to feel very calm, very efficient, and very much in control of the situation. Over her shoulder she said, matter-of-factly, 'Mr Bristow's boat.' She took down a bridle and turned towards him, gathering the reins into loops and knotting them loosely.

Ritchie was staring as if hypnotized. 'Boat?' he echoed hollowly, and extended his hand, robot fashion, to receive the bridle as she thrust it at him. It was her show bridle with the silver inlay work. 'What's this for?' he asked, in the tone of one who doesn't expect an answer.

He got one anyway. 'For Orbit, naturally. When we find him I'm going to ride him home. Put it in Pop's pick-up. I'll bring the saddle.'

Clawing distractedly through his tousled hair with his free hand, Ritchie struggled with his vocal chords until he burst out at last, 'But Mellie, this is crazy! What if you're all wrong? You're only guessing. And even if you're right, I've never *handled* a boat like that.'

Melanie had turned again and was stripping the cover off her show saddle. 'You can drive a car,' she said, 'so you can drive a boat.'

Greeting this firm display of feminine logic with the awed silence it deserved, he tried again. 'Even if I could, how are we going to get to the boat landing?'

'Drive the pick-up.' She swung the softly gleaming saddle to her shoulder with the ease of long practice.

'Gads, Mellie!' Ritchie's voice became falsetto under the stress of emotion. '*I* can't drive it! I've already been arrested once tonight for driving without a licence! They'll – gosh, Mellie – they'll *hang* me!' He paused, brightening. 'Katie's got a permit! Why not get her to –'

'No! There isn't time. And anyway she'd only think of some reason why we shouldn't.' She broke off, glaring furiously at him. 'Ritchie Penfield,' she said ominously, 'are you going to help me rescue Orbit or aren't you? Because if you're not, I'm going to do it by myself, and you can just go fall in a hole and disappear forever!'

Their eyes remained locked in what felt to Melanie like mortal combat for an interval in which Ritchie's face changed expressions at least five times. This virtuoso performance was concluded by the sudden appearance of his familiar, easy grin, and without a word he stepped close, bent, and softly kissed her full on the lips.

It wasn't easy to feel startled, annoyed, and strangely fluttery all at the same moment, but Melanie managed to do so. Fortunately he spared her the necessity of reacting to this unexpected gesture by taking the saddle from her and lifting it to his own shoulder. 'All right,' he said, 'but you'll have to promise me one thing.'

'What?' Melanie asked suspiciously.

'That you'll visit me every day in prison, and bring me cookies and stuff. Come on, let's go start breaking laws.'

As the pick-up rattled along the deserted road, its headlights knifing into the blackness ahead, Melanie's mood of calmness and control threatened to leave her. There were so many uncertainties ahead, so many impossible things that must be done. In her lap she clutched the little canvas bag of oats she had filled at the last minute, and she tried to remember just what it was she had said in the note she had scribbled hastily for Katie and left on the kitchen table. She could feel Ritchie's tenseness as he bent forward over the wheel watching the road intently. There was scarcely a chance in a thousand they would encounter a policeman or anyone else on this lonely back road so late in the night, but if it did happen, if Ritchie were to be caught in this new lawless act on top of all his others, she would never be able to forgive herself. And what if she were wrong after all? What if they were to arrive at the boat landing and find the ugly old houseboat floating peacefully at its mooring with the grey-haired man inside, sleeping the sleep of the innocent?

She stubbornly thrust the thought aside. It simply couldn't be so. Everything had to have happened the way she outlined it in her mind. There was no other explanation. But there were other worrisome thoughts that could not be so easily put aside. What if Ritchie really couldn't run the boat. He had been operating tractors and other farm machinery, including his father's battered old jeep, since he was quite small, and was good at taking them apart and fixing whatever went wrong. But what if boats were entirely different? Further, even if he could work the boat and they did catch up with the houseboat, which by this time had a head start of about five or six hours, what was to happen then? How did you go about taking a houseboat away from a rough-looking man who undoubtedly would not be in favour of the idea?

Melanie clutched her oats bag tighter and felt her body shrink inside Mom's old rust-coloured sweater, which she had snatched from a hook on the basement stair landing along with a jacket of Pop's for Ritchie. The whole undertaking now looked foolhardy, impossibly difficult, and undoubtedly dangerous. She shivered.

In a short time Ritchie slowed the pick-up, switched off the headlights and crept another hundred feet or so with the aid of the parking lights only, before pulling off the road at last.

The rain had stopped but there were neither stars nor moon, and the night around them was impenetrably black. Melanie felt, rather than saw, the darkness close round the cab of the pick-up the instant Ritchie turned all the lights off. There was no sound but the whispering drip of water falling from the trees.

Melanie groped under the dashboard for Pop's flashlight. With the aid of its feeble beam they made their way down the steep incline to the boat landing, speaking in whispers. Not until their feet touched the dock, its worn planks slippery with rain, were they able to see anything at all of the craft moored there. Eagerly but fearfully Melanie's eyes probed ahead, her throat tight with anxiety. Then her free hand gripped Ritchie's arm tightly and she whispered excitedly, 'It's gone! I can see – it's gone!' There was only black emptiness now in the place where the stranger's ungainly old houseboat had been.

They went on beyond the space and turned out on to the little jetty at which a dozen or so small boats were moored. The flashlight's beam pointed them out, one by one. Mr Bristow's boat – long, low and sleek – lay like a hawk among the starlings at the outer end of the jetty. The white canvas cover stretched tight across its cockpit reflected the light like a patch of snow. Painted in silver-white letters on its rakish bow was its name, *Wayfarer*.

Ritchie, looking shapeless and larger than life in Pop's jacket, set the saddle down and knelt at the edge of the dock. 'Hold the light, Mellie,' he said in a low tone, 'so I can get this cover off.'

Once the cover was off, folded and stowed under a thwart at the stern of the cockpit, Ritchie turned quickly to the control panel in front of the left forward seat, leaving Melanie to get the saddle, bridle and feedbag aboard.

Joining him then, Melanie peered with dismay at the array of instruments, gauges, knobs and other mysterious devices to which she couldn't even put a name. 'Oh, golly,' she said uneasily. 'Do you think you can make it run?'

He didn't answer, but went on moving the light from object to object, studying everything carefully. In a minute he took the key she had given him, slid it into a lock and turned it. Braced to hear the motor roar into life, Melanie felt a little let down when nothing happened except that the whole panel suddenly glowed with soft light. Ritchie snapped off the flashlight and slid it into a pocket. Then he began jiggling levers, turning knobs experimentally and bending close to read the small print on the panel. At last he grunted with what sounded like satisfaction and said, still without looking at her, 'There must be oars or a paddle. See if you can find one.'

She scrambled over the back of her seat to look. Finding a paddle secured by a pair of metal clips to the portside gunwale, she brought it forward. 'We'll need it to push off,' Ritchie explained. 'I don't dare start the motor right here; it'd wake up the whole county. We'll have to shove out into the current and drift down a bit, and then – and then start it.'

To Melanie his pause sounded louder than his words. The pause said there was at least a little doubt in Ritchie's mind about his ability to start the engine. Her mind leapt to the falls five miles below the boat landing, where the river tumbled down in boiling anger over a 100-foot cliff.

He must have been reading her mind, for he said quickly, 'If I can't start it we can get it to shore somehow, with the paddle. Or if we can't, we can always swim ashore.'

'And just – let the boat go?' Melanie asked, horrified.

'If we have to.'

'Oh, golly! It must be worth an awful lot of money.'

'For a guess,' Ritchie said, 'about six or seven thousand bucks.' He hunched his shoulders purposefully. 'But never mind all that; I'll start it or bust. Give me the paddle, and you scramble up on the bow and untie.'

She obeyed orders and scrambled back into the front seat as Ritchie, standing in the stern, placed the tip of the paddle against the nearest boat and gave a mighty shove.

Slowly, ponderously, *Wayfarer*'s stern swung out away from the dock. Ritchie paddled furiously, the stern swung farther, and in a few moments Melanie felt the current grip the boat. She glanced up and, as if she were watching some strange slow-motion film, saw the dock, the row of boats, and the shadowy hulks of the houseboats beyond move away from her, growing ever more formless and unreal until they disappeared altogether in the darkness. The only sounds were those of Ritchie's heavy breathing as he laboured to drive the craft still further towards the centre of the stream, the faint lapping of water along the boat's smooth hull, and the beating of her own heart.

Soon he came scrambling forward, brushing unceremoniously against her as he climbed into the pilot's seat. 'Okay,' he said, making no effort now to keep his voice down. 'Keep your fingers crossed.'

She did keep them crossed, and after the starter had broken into its whining sound three or four times with no result, she said a desperate little prayer. Again the starter whirred and whined. Again nothing happened. She had the feeling that the boat had swung round and was drifting downstream, stern first. How fast there was no way of knowing. And what if they were to run into something, or run aground on a bank at the next curve of the river.

The same thought must have occurred to Ritchie, because he spoke suddenly, still without taking his eyes off the control panel. 'Grab the paddle and go to the stern. Here, take the flashlight. If you see anything to shove against, shove!'

Kneeling on the upholstered thwart, Melanie felt very much alone and not at all efficient as she grasped the paddle with one hand and aimed the flashlight with the other. Its beam penetrated the darkness a few yards beyond the jaunty little jackstaff which pointed upward and rearward, flagless now, from *Wayfarer*'s blunt stern. She could see water, black and oily-looking in the yellow beam, but nothing more.

Once more the starter whined, went dead, whined again, coughed, spluttered, threatened to die; and then it came to thunderous life, splitting the ears with a roar. The whole boat – Melanie with it – trembled and shook, and for a horrible moment she wondered if Ritchie had punched the wrong button and twisted the wrong knob. But if he had, he quickly corrected it, for the roar slackened, rose once again, and then died down to a throaty, businesslike hum.

Melanie turned to look. Just as she did, Ritchie pulled another switch and the black night vanished as powerful twin headlamps flashed on, lighting a broad path ahead. She dropped her paddle to the deck and scrambled forward into the leather seat beside him. 'You *did* it!' she exulted.

She might as well have said nothing at all. Ritchie was lost in an ecstasy of his own. With a reverent look he cautiously did something to a little lever and the engine responded with a deeper, even throatier hum. 'Listen to it, Mellie!' he burst out. 'Just listen! It sounds like a thousand horses in that engine. Wow!'

'Well, then,' said Melanie, who could get excited about horses but not about horsepower, 'let's get going.'

'Okay,' Ritchie said, sounding a little doubtful but giving the bill of his baseball cap a determined tug, 'hang on to your hat.' He moved the gear lever, advanced the throttle cautiously, and Melanie suddenly felt herself pushed back against the seat as the propeller bit into the water, arresting the drifting motion of the boat and sending it plunging forward. Ritchie, crouched tensely over the wheel, looked as wearily grim as if he were driving a team of tigers in harness.

A few moments later, the boat landing they had just left appeared suddenly in the glare of the probing headlights. They were heading straight for it. Ritchie cramped the wheel to the left, and *Wayfarer*, accustomed to a lighter touch, slewed and skittered sideways in an effort to turn at a right angle, flailing the water into a creamy wake behind her. The manoeuvre sent Melanie sliding against the gunwale with a jarring thump. By the time she straightened up, Ritchie had yanked the throttle farther open than he intended, and the *Wayfarer* lunged forward like a rowelled horse. Now the headlights showed she was aimed like an arrow for the opposite shore, a high, shadowy wall of trees and undergrowth. Again Ritchie spun the wheel and again *Wayfarer* skittered and bucked.

So it went for the first five minutes or so. An observer ashore, had there been one, would have sworn that a drunken man or a dangerous lunatic was loose on the river in a high-powered motor launch. None of Ritchie's experience in handling motor vehicles had prepared him for *Wayfarer*'s sensitive, hair-trigger responses. It was as if a child who had never ridden anything but a bored, weary, stubborn carnival pony were suddenly to be placed on Orbit's back and handed the reins.

Soon, however, it became obvious that, bit by bit, Ritchie was gaining mastery over his runaway steed. He seemed to know by instinct just how to correct his mistakes. *Wayfarer*'s course and speed became gradually less erratic, and soon she was humming smoothly along, turning only enough to follow the gentle bends of the river between its tree-crowded banks.

Ritchie turned to Melanie at last, and his grin flashed white in the soft light of the instrument panel. 'You still here?' he said. 'Thought I'd bucked you off about a mile back.'

'Not a chance.' Melanie glanced apprehensively into the darkness astern. 'All that uproar,' she said. 'I saw lights go on. We must have awakened the whole state.'

Ritchie shrugged. 'Nothing they can do about it.' He made a minute adjustment of the boat's direction, peering through the broad wind-and-spray screen above the instrument panel. Then he breathed, 'Golly, what a dream of a boat.'

Melanie turned and looked behind, where, naturally, there was nothing to be seen but darkness. 'How far do you suppose we've come?'

'Not very far, if you mean *up* the river. *Across* it we've gone about a hundred miles – by the way I feel, anyhow.'

'You tired?' Melanie asked.

He shook his head, not very convincingly. 'Even if I was, you couldn't get me to quit piloting this dreamboat for a mil – ' He broke off and threw her a quick glance. 'But you must be dead! I did sleep some, but you didn't, and it must be about four o'clock. Why don't you just curl up on the seat and – '

Melanie shook her head. 'I couldn't sleep. And anyway, I have to help watch. What if we were to pass the houseboat in the dark and not even see it?'

Ritchie snorted loudly. 'In *this* river? Gosh, Mellie, you couldn't even pass a *rowboat* in this river without seeing it. Go on and lie down for a while. There's nothing you can do, and there's no telling how long it'll take to catch up with them.'

Melanie resisted. The thought of sleep hadn't occurred to her; but now that Ritchie had suggested it, it began to be a powerful attraction. Soon it would be twenty-four hours since she had last slept, and so much had happened since then that it seemed a lifetime away. Grudgingly she gave in.

She lay down on the capacious leather seat, pulling Mom's old sweater as far up around her neck as it would go, pillowing her head on the sack of oats. It wasn't very soft, but it smelled like Orbit. Almost instantly the deep hum of the motor and its gentle vibrations became an irresistible lullaby, and sleep drew near.

'Ritchie,' she said, making a tremendous effort to say anything at all. 'How long do you think it will be till we catch up?'

'I've been working it out,' he replied. 'They couldn't be making more than three or four miles an hour, dragging that old houseboat upriver, and they've probably been gone about six hours. So that would make it somewhere around twenty miles. In the dark like this we can't go much faster, and it'll be dark for another hour yet, but once it's daylight I can open this thing up, and . . .'

But Melanie had dropped into a soundless sea of sleep.

Not even a fragment of a dream intruded. Time stopped. When it started again, her shoulder was being shaken urgently, and Ritchie's voice, squeaky with excitement, was saying, 'I spotted it, Mellie! The houseboat! About a mile ahead!'

Chapter 15

HER eyes snapped open and she sat up. There was a world around her now, a green world split down the middle by the misty river – and the sun was sweeping the tips of the loftiest fir trees high above.

'I just rounded into this straight stretch,' Ritchie hurried on, 'and caught a glimpse – I'm sure I did – as it disappeared round the next bend.'

Melanie peered ahead but saw only the empty river, its walls of trees broken now and then by clearings filled with houses and barns. They were passing a clearing now, on the right. On a rickety-looking pier at the water's edge two little boys looked up from their play and waved. Her throat went suddenly dry. The time was almost on them, the time when they would have to do something, and she hadn't the least idea what they were going to do.

'And Mellie – ' she caught a worried note in Ritchie's voice, ' – we're getting awful low on petrol.'

It took a moment for this appalling information to sink in. Melanie wasn't accustomed to thinking about motor vehicles and what made them run. They simply ran when you wanted them to and stood still when you didn't. But now her mind leapt to the unbearable thought of this powerful boat just suddenly quitting and the two of them sitting, helpless as a pair of floating chips, while Orbit was borne off once more to his unknown and frightening destination.

'I didn't think to check on it until a while ago,' Ritchie went on apologetically, as if it were all his fault. 'The gauge is right on the empty mark.'

Melanie glanced automatically at the instrument panel, which told her nothing at all. Then she half stood for a better view of the river ahead. *Wayfarer* was sliding along now at a speed that sent twin waves rolling out from her bow in an ever-widening 'V' shape. The next bend in the river seemed to be rushing swiftly towards them.

Ritchie glanced up and motioned for her to bend down where he could make himself more easily heard over the sound of the engine. He talked rapidly. 'I had a plan, Mellie, and it might work if we had plenty of petrol. But now we can't take a chance. So here's what we'll do – ' He paused. 'Unless you can think of something better.'

Melanie shook her head positively.

'Okay,' Ritchie went on, 'I'll ease up behind the houseboat. The guy towing it won't see us because the houseboat will be in between, and he won't hear us because his own motor will be making a lot of racket. So you can jump aboard and start doing whatever you've got to do about Orbit while I – ' he swallowed visibly, 'while I do whatever I have to do.'

She nodded, then said apprehensively, 'What – what *will* you do?'

'Cut his tow rope. Ease up as close behind him as I can, cut it, and hitch it to this boat, then tow the houseboat ashore as quick as I can and tie it up somehow. After that we can think what to do next.'

'But – but Ritchie, what will the man be doing during all this?'

'Heading for shore and running like crazy, if he's got any sense.'

'But what if he doesn't? Oh, Ritchie, there's no telling what he – '

'Never mind all that; I'll handle him one way or another,' he said with a confidence she knew was false. Suddenly he flung up his arm to point. 'There! There it is, Mellie!'

They had just swept round a sharp bend and there, scarcely a hundred yards ahead, was the grey, ungainly rear end of the old houseboat, wallowing along like a chicken coop adrift in a flood. 'Quick!' Ritchie barked. 'Get up on the bow. Don't jump till I shove right up against it.' He eased back on the throttle until *Wayfarer* slowed to what, for her, was a crawl.

Scooping up the feedbag and bridle, Melanie took a deep breath and swung a leg over the gunwale and down to the narrow catwalk that offered a precarious foothold on the side of *Wayfarer* just above the waterline.

It was like crawling out of the front seat of an automobile on to its radiator while the car was in motion, except that there was no door to be dealt with. There was only the swept-back windscreen to get round, and for handholds there were metal bollards used for mooring lines.

Once round the windscreen, she scrambled up and lay flat, inching her way forward on the highly-polished surface. Now the houseboat's broad, blunt stern loomed high above her, and suddenly she caught her breath. The smell! Clear, un-mistakable, familiar on the fresh morning air was the smell of horse. Every lingering, nagging doubt vanished. Orbit was there – and she was getting closer to him by the second!

Clutching the feedbag and bridle tightly with one arm and hand, she steadied herself with the other against the smooth surface of *Wayfarer*'s bow, and cautiously gathered her feet under her.

She could almost reach up and touch the battered railing at the houseboat's stern. The smell of Orbit was strong now, and she forgot everything else.

Gently, with a muffled little thump, the two craft came together. She turned and flashed a look at Ritchie through the windscreen. He nodded violently. She turned, got lightly to her feet, and without a thought about what might happen if she missed, sprang upward, her free hand grasping for the rail above.

It was easier than climbing on Orbit bareback, and in a moment she stood on the deck in the cramped space between the rail and the boat's rear wall. Glancing back and down, she saw the stretch of water growing wider between the houseboat and *Wayfarer* as Ritchie eased the throttle and let the boat drop back. Soon he would veer off and speed past the plodding old hulk to attempt the mission he had assigned himself.

As she looked, he let go of the wheel and clasped his hands above his head in the fighter's victory salute. She threw him a quick wave, caught the flash of his grin, then turned and hurried along the railing to the door at the forward end of the houseboat.

The door was a large heavy one, suspended from a roller track like the door to the stable at home. Like everything else about the old vessel, the door was in a sad state of repair. It sagged, scraping against the deck at the bottom, and it took every bit of Melanie's strength to drag it far enough open to slip through.

Inside, where the smell of horse was strong, she paused, her heart thumping painfully, while her eyes grew accustomed to the deep gloom. It was as if a piece of the night were trapped in the big box-like room, illuminated only by a pair of small, dirty windows high on each side wall. Peering, she probed the room with her eyes, eagerly at first, then with frantic dismay.

She saw no Orbit – no horse at all. There was a collection of cheap shabby furniture, cupboards and a closet along one wall, a sink and draining-board on the other. At the far end was what appeared to be a blank wall made of new lumber. Near it a few boards lay scattered about.

At that moment, from outside came a burst of sound – the crescendo of *Wayfarer*'s engine as Ritchie opened the throttle. The sound was followed on the instant by another, louder one that seemed to pierce her ears and sweep through her whole body like a flame. Vibrant, unmistakable, it was the shivery, bugling cry of a stallion. It was Orbit! He had scented her – and he was calling!

An answering cry burst from her and she started forward only to whirl a second later as yet a third sound blasted its

156

way into her consciousness. It was a man's voice raised in a startled exclamation.

As the sounds crackled in the stale air, Melanie's horrified eyes made out a figure as it rose from a bedraggled couch in the shadowy corner to the left of the door by which she had entered. She caught only a glimpse of a face, but it was a glimpse in no way comforting. It was the face of a young man of perhaps twenty and it wore the slack-lipped, cunning look of the very stupid.

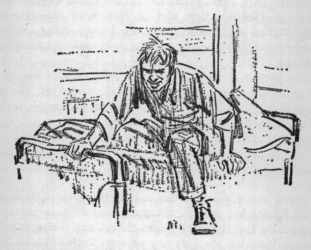

Melanie looked wildly around for something – anything – that could be a weapon. The oatbag dropped from beneath her arm and her right hand tightened around the silver-studded bridle. Again Orbit's ear-piercing call resounded in the narrow space. There was no sound of his movement, though, and by this time Melanie knew why. The part of her mind that was beyond amazement, fear, and dismay had seized on fragments of evidence supplied by her eyes and put them together. The thing that looked like a wall made of new boards was actually a simple but effective squeeze cage. Its principle was the same as the cages she had read about which were used by lion trainers when they needed to immobilize their animals to give them injections or other treatment. In this case, Orbit's kidnappers had built a sort of movable wooden wall, with heavy braces extending out from the bottom. They had led him in his drugged state to a position against the forward bulkhead of the houseboat, shoved their movable wall against him, and nailed the braces to the deck. A few two-by-fours nailed from wall to wall – particularly one right above the back of his neck while his head was held low – would prevent him from kicking, rearing, or moving in any way. And he wouldn't be hurt at all. There would be no scars to mar his beauty when they sold him, or whatever it was they planned.

She backed off another step, her flying fingers sorting out by touch the straps of the heavy bridle and reins. Her arm came slowly back. She was holding the bridle now by the chin strap, the face and head sections hanging free.

She watched the man's eyes, saw them flicker the instant before he lunged, and with all her strength she lashed at his face with the bridle.

Motor idling, *Wayfarer* lay dead in the water while Ritchie Penfield watched Melanie disappear round the corner of the houseboat. The distance between the two craft widened as the big one lumbered along its way upriver. Ritchie twisted round to look in the cockpit behind him in case a spare can of petrol might have materialized there since the last time he looked. None had. With a last despairing look at the fuel gauge, he gripped the wheel firmly, and slid back the throttle.

Wayfarer surged forward and swept quickly abreast of the wallowing houseboat, and there Ritchie's hand faltered on the throttle as he peered ahead.

What caused his faltering was not the sight of the weathered old motor-boat with a shapeless figure hunched over its wheel; it was the tow rope. It wasn't a rope at all – it was a steel cable. His plan was doomed before he could even attempt to execute it.

But he had to do something, and do it fast. Any moment now he would be seen, and any moment *Wayfarer*'s mighty voice would cough and die. The fuel gauge needle was lying motionless at the 'empty' mark. There would be time, perhaps, for one move: to force the man to run aground. What followed would have to take care of itself. He opened the throttle a little and *Wayfarer* slid forward, humming a throatier tune, her rakish bows pointed straight at the man in the boat.

A second passed, then another, and then the slumping figure jerked erect; his head, in a dark, shapeless hat, snapped round, and Ritchie glimpsed a grimace of astonishment and alarm on an unshaven face. Then the man went into action, frantically spinning his wheel to the right, towards the shore. The old boat's bow moved sluggishly to the right. With the drag of the houseboat resisting any movement, it could do nothing in a hurry.

Wayfarer hurtled closer. Ritchie saw the man's mouth stretch wide in a snag-toothed yell but could hear nothing above the noise of his engine. All but on top of the other boat now, he wrenched his wheel to the left, and *Wayfarer* slid sideways, digging her churning propeller deep as she clawed her way back towards the centre of the river, missing a collision by inches.

Ritchie's head snapped round in time to see the other boat pitch and rock violently in the wave of *Wayfarer*'s passing. Then he swung in a wide circle to the left. If only the fuel would hold out for another pass!

It did. *Wayfarer* went rocketing in again. But this time Ritchie miscalculated, hesitated a split second too long before pulling *Wayfarer* into a foaming turn. She turned, but not until there was a sound like a distant rifle shot and a bone-cracking jar that rocked Ritchie from ankles to neck. Again his head snapped round as *Wayfarer* leapt away. This time he saw the man wildly clawing the air, his hands torn from the wheel, his body slamming sideways against the side of his boat.

Ritchie swung in a circle again, watching, gauging distance and direction.

The man appeared to have righted himself and taken the wheel again, but there was something wrong with him. He seemed to be slumping in an attitude of weariness. His hat was gone, and his grizzled head made an excellent bull's-eye. His boat was closer to shore now. One more pass – just one more . . .

Ritchie suddenly froze, all but letting go of the controls. Something had suddenly appeared on the little foredeck of the houseboat. It was a person – no, *two* persons! They were doing some grotesque sort of dance. One wore a rust-coloured sweater. Melanie and a man!

Ritchie exploded into action. Leaping to his feet and yanking the throttle wide open in the same instant, Ritchie steered the roaring, racing *Wayfarer* first with one hand and then the other while he tore his way out of the cumbersome jacket, swept the old baseball cap from his head and kicked off his shoes.

About a hundred yards of water lay between *Wayfarer* and her objective, and she gulped up the distance as a screaming jet gulps air. The man in the boat watched her coming, his whiskery face a mask of terror. Ritchie's bare feet gripped the edge of *Wayfarer*'s gunwale as he crouched behind the windscreen, guiding his waterborne projectile with one hand. On it went, straight for the mark. Eighty feet . . . sixty feet . . . fifty feet . . .

Ritchie dived. With the gunwale for a springboard, he gave a mighty thrust with his legs and arched outward towards the boiling foam of *Wayfarer*'s wake. There was a wild scream and a sickening, splintering crash, but Ritchie heard neither, for the river rose beneath his flying body and slapped him like a mighty paddle in the stomach, chest and face.

In the middle of a green meadow that sloped to the river's edge a few hundred feet upstream, a man who had been sitting open-mouthed on his tractor for the last few minutes came suddenly to life, scrambled down and started for his house at full pelt, yelling as he went, 'Helen, Helen! Quick! Get the sheriff on the phone!'

Chapter 16

FOR Melanie, those first few minutes inside the old houseboat turned into a nightmare of violence so terrifying and so bewilderingly fast that, later, she was able to remember the details of it, when she remembered them at all, only dimly. It became like a horror movie she had gone to, and through two-thirds of which she had sat with her eyes tight shut and her fingers in her ears.

There were confused recollections of striking with her bridle at a looming face, of hatefully muscular arms closing on her, lifting her, propelling her through the door and out on to the deck, of her own breath coming in sobs as she uselessly fought with all her strength. There was the roaring of a boat engine somewhere near by and, more clearly than anything else, the sound of Orbit's scream, and the sharp report of cracking wood as he struggled, maddened by terror, to break loose from his cage.

What was suddenly beautifully clear was that all at once the rough arms let her go, the man grunted with something like consternation, leapt to the rail and stood there with his broad back towards her. She didn't know that he had caught sight of *Wayfarer*, throttle wide open, roaring straight towards him. All she knew was that suddenly she was free, that Orbit stood in desperate need of her, and that there in front of her was the unguarded back of her tormentor.

She didn't think, she merely acted. Like a sprinter off at the starting gun, she launched herself forward. At the last possible instant she ducked her head and her feet left the deck as she hurled herself, a small but potent battering ram, dead-centre into the target.

The impact wrenched her neck cruelly and she flopped gasping to the deck, but she managed to roll to one side and look up in time to see a wildly clawing figure topple over the railing and disappear from sight. Then she picked herself up and dashed for the cabin door.

Behind her came a screeching, ripping, splintering crash, and the old boat lurched and shuddered. She didn't even turn to look. Only one thing in the world was important now. In the gloom of the cabin she fought to bring her gasping breath under control as she called out, 'Orbit boy, easy now, eeeeasy! It's me. I'm here – and everything's going to be all right.'

For a few horrible seconds Ritchie wondered if he were going to lie helplessly face down in the water until he drowned, unable to move a hand or foot to save himself. His brain knew perfectly well how swimming should be done and it kept telling his muscles to get at the job. But they refused. He simply lay there while deafening noises thundered aimlessly round in his head and the whole front of him ached with arrogant, demanding pain. He was stunned and temporarily paralysed by the shock of striking a solid sheet of water after travelling through the air at something like thirty miles an hour.

His brain also kept trying to tell him there was something else he ought to be doing – something terribly urgent. But the message wasn't getting through. Fortunately, the body often can operate without the help of the brain, and all at once his head rolled over, air rushed into his famished lungs with a sound like a sob, and his hands and feet began moving.

A second later the message arrived. Melanie! He had to rescue her! He began to dogpaddle, feebly but with determination, keeping himself afloat until his head cleared and the pain subsided.

At first he found himself peering towards a stretch of totally unfamiliar river-bank, its greenery broken only by a ledge of crumbling rock. He turned himself round, stared, kicked madly with his feet until he rose high in the water like a fish standing on its tail, and stared again. Then, without losing another moment, he struck out with his swift crawl stroke.

What he had seen, about 150 feet upstream and close in to the shore, was the old houseboat slowly pivoting on her stern and swinging broadside to the river's current, her bow encumbered by a pair of boats that appeared to be locked together in a crazy embrace. What he didn't know, and hadn't time to think about, was that *Wayfarer*, owing to some freak of current, speed, and direction, had veered to starboard at the very instant of his desperate dive, and instead of striking the other boat amidship had struck it a glancing blow at the stern and proceeded to ride up and nearly over the towing cable behind it, tearing her bottom out in the process.

Even if Ritchie had known all this, it wouldn't have made any difference. What set him to swimming as he had never swum before was the glimpse of a head and a pair of arms flailing madly at the water just below and beyond the houseboat's stern. There could be only one explanation for this: the unknown man who had been struggling with Mellie on the deck had thrown her overboard. Worse than that, he must have injured her so that she could not swim. That Melanie might have thrown the *man* in the river was not a possibility that would have occurred to anybody in his right mind.

The distance narrowed more quickly than he thought and soon he was within hailing distance of the struggling figure. He was debating whether or not to waste precious breath calling a word of encouragement when he glimpsed an upraised arm and a hand that groped desperately along the hull of the houseboat, seeking something to hang on to. It wasn't Melanie's hand!

Ritchie stopped swimming. He could see the head now, and part of a face. It was a man! A man who could swim barely enough to keep himself afloat.

Where, then, was Melanie? He looked wildly around. There was no one else in the water. Could the man have drowned her? That was impossible. This floundering swimmer couldn't have drowned anybody, least of all Melanie, who could swim like an otter.

But where could she be? Abruptly Ritchie struck out for the houseboat. He had no hope of finding her there, but at the moment he could think of nothing else to do.

Passing within ten feet of the flailing, grasping man in the water, who appeared to be struggling towards the shore, Ritchie barely glanced at him. The man could drown, for all he cared. In a few moments he reached the low stern of the houseboat and heaved himself aboard.

He stood there, dripping, letting his breath catch up with him. His right ear made a scratchy, subterranean sound and he shook his head to get the water out. That was when he heard a voice. He froze, all but his head and eyes, which turned involuntarily and foolishly upward as if the sound had come from the sky. It hadn't, of course. It had come from inside the houseboat. Ritchie listened, stunned and unbelieving.

It was Melanie's voice, and she was talking steadily in a gentle, high-pitched, sing-song way. 'Isn't it a nice boat ride, Orbit? Yes indeed, we're having a reeeeel nice boat ride, and after a while if you be good I'll get you out of there. And besides I've got some nice oats here, and . . .'

Over Ritchie's face, unknown to him, spread a silly, rapturous, utterly idiotic grin.

Fears of every description slithered around the edges of Melanie's mind, watchful for an opening; but with fierce resolution she kept them at bay. And she talked. She talked quietly, soothingly, and incessantly in the silly sing-song Orbit loved so well.

To prattle away, allowing her voice to betray no hint of the fears that shouted inside her, was perhaps the most difficult thing she had ever done. Foremost among the terrors was the thought that at any moment the man might appear again. She hadn't even looked to see what had become of him; and while she passionately hoped he had sunk like a stone to the bottom of the river, there was no very convincing reason to believe he had. And the other man – the one running the boat. She had hardly given him a thought, but he must be around somewhere, doing something. Then, of course, there was Ritchie. All she knew about him was that there had been a tremendous amount of roaring and crashing going on, for which Ritchie seemed in some way to be responsible. So now there was another fear to add to all the rest – that he had been badly hurt, or even killed in the midst of all that crashing. And it was all her fault, every bit of it.

Fortunately she was spared yet another fear for the merciful reason that it hadn't occurred to her to think about it: in the grip of the river's current the old houseboat was drifting ponderously downriver, reluctantly accompanied by two boats, one of them rapidly filling with water, and both of them inextricably tangled in twenty feet of towing cable.

Fears or no fears, Melanie talked, and while she talked she worked. She was perched now on the top of the barricade that held Orbit pressed against the wall. The squeeze-box cage was built very much as she had envisaged it, except that instead of a board nailed across it just above his neck there was a double length of heavy rope stapled to both sides of the cage and knotted in the middle. The rope held his head down to within about three feet of the floor, cruelly but successfully preventing him from even starting to rear. All she could see of him was his back and the beginning of his mane at the withers. Until she got the rope loose he couldn't lift his head to look at her and feel the stroke of her hand along his muzzle and be comforted.

Putting one hand on his withers, she found his coat drenched in the sweat of his fear, and he trembled unceasingly. With that hand she went on stroking and patting, and with the other she began on the knots. The sound of her voice never stopped.

The task was impossible. In hours of straining his neck

against the rope, trying desperately to raise his head, Orbit had wrenched the knots so tight that no human fingers could have loosened them. There was nothing to do but cut the rope, and Melanie had no knife.

'Mellie!' Ritchie's voice came softly through the side of the houseboat's cabin. 'Mellie!'

For a second Melanie forgot to keep talking. She was frightened. On top of everything else, she was starting to hear voices that weren't there.

'Mellie!' came the voice again. 'It's me!'

'Oh – *Ritchie*!'

On the other side of the wall the voice sounded tremulous

with all manner of flattering emotions, and the smile on Ritchie's face grew even broader. Then the voice said, 'Well, come on in here – quick. I need your knife!'

At the very moment this tender exchange was going on, there were other exchanges in progress at separate points many miles away. For one, the radio dispatcher in the county sheriff's office was having trouble with an excited man on the telephone.

'*Piracy!*' the dispatcher was saying. 'Attack on a *house-boat*! Now slow down a minute, mister. Take it from the beginning. . . . Yeah – yeah – got it. . . . Give me that location again, mister. . . . And your name and address. . . . Right. . . . Sure we'll look into it. Right away. . . . And mister, is there a boat landing near there? We may want to borrow a boat. . . . Right – got it. Thanks for calling.'

Another exchange was taking place in an office of the State Highway Patrol where a grey-haired officer was speaking into a telephone in the flat, unemotional tones of a man who has already heard everything at least twice. He kept making notes on a pad of paper as he talked. On the pad was pencilled in blunt, blocky letters the words, 'WEBB, Kathleen. 7.08 a.m. Missing – WEBB, Melanie. PENFIELD, R.' Into the phone he was saying, 'Yes, Miss Webb. No, Miss Webb, Officer Murdock went off duty at six. . . . I understand, Miss Webb, the horse is on the houseboat. . . . No, Miss Webb, I do not think you are off your rocker. . . . Oh, you *are* off your rocker. Beg pardon, Miss Webb. . . . Of course, we will. Right away. Now you just relax and – No, *I* will not relax; *you* relax. Good-bye, Miss Webb.'

When the officer hung up he made a few more notes and looked up to meet the eyes of a young newspaper reporter who said ecstatically, 'Did I hear what I thought I heard?'

'They're your ears,' the officer said. 'Scram now, will you? I've got hoss-thieves to catch.' He flipped a switch on a little metal box on his desk and started talking into it, fast.

The reporter stood staring into space as though communing with unseen, benevolent spirits. 'Horse-thieves!' he murmured rapturously. 'Kids! A houseboat!' He dashed for his telephone in the press room.

Not until Ritchie entered the gloomy cabin did he realize how bright it was outside, how far the sun had risen during his mad explosion of activity on the river. He had to stare hard to see that Melanie had acquired an ugly bruise on one cheek and a torn shirt since he last saw her. There were scores of questions he wanted to ask, but there wasn't time. 'Orbit all right?' he asked, handing her his knife.

She took it. 'I think so,' she said, looking anxiously into his face, which was streaming with river water. 'Is – is everything all right?'

'Well – ' He groped for a way to reassure her without actually lying. 'Well – it's *going* to be.' He started back to the door and paused. 'I'll be back, Mellie, quick as I can. And don't worry about that – that guy. He won't bother you any more.'

Out on the deck again, Ritchie's eyes caught a flash of movement to his right, along the river's edge about thirty yards upstream. It was a man – no, two men. One on the shore, the other in the water. The first, grizzled and hatless, with one arm hanging useless at his side, was struggling to pull the other from the river.

Obviously, there was nothing further to fear from that pair. He stared at them with contemptuous indifference, then turned quickly away. There were plenty of other things to fear. He had to work out what could be done, and then do it fast. The river wasn't going to wait for him.

Chapter 17

IT was just as well for Melanie that she couldn't see what Ritchie was doing for the next thirty minutes or glimpse what was going on in his mind as hope after hope rose up only to be crushed by reality, giving way at last to desperation.

First he swam to the tangle of boats and cable, trying not to look at *Wayfarer*, which lay wedged between houseboat and tow-boat, kept afloat only by the cable, which was jammed into her rudder and propeller. His object was to start the tow-boat, which appeared relatively undamaged, and tow the houseboat to shore.

That was the first hope to be dashed. He found the old boat ankle-deep in petrol from its ruptured tank. He didn't dare to try to start the motor. One spark from the ignition system could incinerate him in a blast of flame.

The next hope was to swim ashore with enough rope to tie round a tree and halt the big craft's helpless drift. But there was no rope in the boat. All his frantic searching failed to turn up so much as a foot of it. A still more frantic search in the wreck of the *Wayfarer* was rewarded by a twenty-foot length, new and bright, but wholly inadequate. He needed fifty feet, at the barest minimum.

Even if Melanie had known about all of this, there was absolutely nothing she could have done about it; and in any case her hands were far too full with Orbit. Talking steadily, she sawed through the taut neck rope. He parted its last few strands himself, throwing his head aloft as if it were on giant springs, the whites of his eyes red-veined and wild, his lips darkened and matted with foam from his mouth. The sight of him turned her eyes hot with tears, but she kept her voice steady as she slid her arms round his neck and hugged and went on talking.

The next task was to free him altogether, and there was no way to do it but to take the cage apart, board by board.

Leaving Orbit long enough to snatch up a hammer she had seen lying where it had been carelessly tossed to the deck, she fitted its claw to a protruding nail and tugged. Nothing happened. She tugged harder, harder still, and then with all her strength. The nail gave at last and came out with a horrible screeching sound. But there were more nails – dozens of them – and it was desperately hard work to pull nails and keep talking to Orbit at the same time.

If only Ritchie would come back! And why didn't he? What was he doing, anyway? She squashed the petulant questions instantly. Whatever he was doing was something that had to be done. '. . . So I guess I'll just have to pull some more nails, Orbit. And please don't jump every time, even if it is a perfectly awful noise. I can't help it and I'm only trying to . . .'

She raised her head quickly as Ritchie appeared suddenly in the doorway, but her smile of relief died when she got a look at his face. River water was streaming down it, he was panting for breath, and his grin was a mask of anxiety. He was badly worried.

His eyes shifted from side to side, desperately searching. 'Mellie – you seen any rope around? Got to have more rope.'

It was she, her eyes more accustomed to the gloom of the cabin, who spotted the coil of greyed and greasy rope where it lay half under the sagging bed in the far corner. He grabbed it up with a look of profound relief and hurried out again, mumbling something about being safe on shore in no time.

Melanie paused in her monologue long enough to take a very deep breath, and doggedly attacked the next nail.

In the houseboat, where a narrow ray from the ascending sun crept slowly across the floor as the boat swung in the current, then stopped and crawled back the way it had come, Melanie suddenly broke off her endless, crazily cheerful monologue and raised her head, peering at Orbit. His ears had snapped forward and he had stopped nibbling at her arm with his lips.

He was free now. Pulling, heaving, wrenching, putting more into the labour than she really had to give, she had managed to remove five of the boards from the side of the cage and persuaded Orbit to step over the remaining two. She had bridled him quickly, the better to control him, and was now engaged in sumultaneously calming him further and rubbing down his sweat-matted coat with her old sweater.

Seeing his ears move forward, she listened. At first she heard nothing but the vacuum of silence left when her voice stopped. She wondered yet again, and this time with greater uneasiness, just where Ritchie was and what he was doing. It was an odd and lonely feeling, being shut up in this huge box which she knew was moving, though it gave no feeling of motion. Time, too, was moving on, though it seemed to have been standing still forever.

Then she heard what Orbit heard and resisted straightening with a start. The sound was faint, muffled by the walls around her, but it was unmistakably a motor-boat. She straightened slowly, straining her ears. The boat was swiftly coming near. Her mind raced. The noise! It would set Orbit off again, just when she was getting him really calm!

Moving slowly, holding her urgency in check, she patted his neck once more and said, 'you're not going to be a big baby and get scared again, *are* you? I've got to step outside – but I'll be right back, and after that we're going to get out of this nasty old thing and go home . . .'

She moved across to the door, and with a final word of reassurance stepped outside. At first she saw nothing but the river-bank, then she got her bearings and stepped round the corner of the cabin.

The oncoming boat was the first thing she saw. She jumped to the rail, found the torn and dirty sweater still in her hands and waved it frantically to attract attention. Then she raised her hands, palms outward, and made violent pushing signals. Her lips and throat – all of her vocal apparatus except the voice itself – yelled, 'Stop! Slow down! Stay away! You'll scare him – you'll scare him!'

The boat came on straight as an arrow, and in the very midst of all these wild gyrations a new thought came blasting into her frantic brain. Ritchie! Where in the awful world was *Ritchie*?

Her eyes swept the river one way, then back – and then she saw him. He was nothing but a head of yellow hair glistening in the sunlight about two hundred feet ahead and to the left of the drifting houseboat, and a pair of arms that were lifting themselves out of the water in a dogged rhythm – first one, then the other – and dropping into it again.

In the same shattering instant Melanie knew both what he was trying to do and that he was too weak to do it. She didn't stop to think, so she would never know what decision she would have made if she had. Orbit's safety, or Ritchie's. Still waving signals towards the approaching boat, she did a frenzied dance: left toe to right heel, right toe to left heel, stripping the boots from her feet. Then she jumped to the rail. Even as she stood poised for an instant there was time for the thought that if she delayed for just a second or two, waving madly, the boat people would get the idea. They would stop. They wouldn't frighten Orbit into harming himself. But she couldn't delay. Whatever might happen, she couldn't delay. Ritchie was in trouble. He was in bad trouble.

Her slim body shot away from the rail in a flat racing dive, and she was swimming as she hit the water.

Three minutes later, as the motor of the red launch died to a mutter and it glided the last few yards towards the two splashing figures, the three men aboard were able to make out at last just what sort of people they were about to rescue. They saw a dark-haired girl swimming sidestroke with one hand and with the other towing a boy twice her size by means of a handful of yellow hair.

To judge by what the men heard in the silence that followed the cutting of the motor, the girl was not at all pleased with the boy. 'You are *not* all right, Ritchie Penfield!' they heard her say, panting with the exertion of swimming for two. 'Now – will – you – shut – *up*!'

Chapter 18

EVEN on a quiet river, news has a way of getting around. Not long after the sheriff's officers in the red launch had plucked the exhausted Ritchie from the river, asked a few questions of Melanie, and taken the houseboat in tow, a sheriff's patrol car cruising slowly along the river road a short distance upstream came to a sudden halt. Its driver had spotted two men in sodden clothing as they tried to take cover behind a heap of fallen timber. Hand on his pistol butt, the officer herded the dispirited pair into the back seat of the car, questioned them briefly, and then spent several minutes talking into his radio.

A short while later, about two hundred miles to the south, a heavy-set, youngish man in battered cowboy boots walked out of a roadside café, wiping his mouth with the back of his hand, and started towards his car to which was hitched a trailer with a palomino mare inside. In the parking area he was joined by a state highway patrolman who took him by the arm in an almost friendly fashion and said, 'Let's go in my car, shall we, mister?'

In the newsroom of the *Oregon Daily* in Portland the city editor was talking to a man with a camera case slung from his shoulder while a young woman stood by, waiting her turn. 'A couple of miles west of Cascade,' he was saying to the photographer. 'At the boat landing. Dawes'll meet you there.'

Then he turned to the young woman. 'You cover all the horsey doings, don't you? Ever run across a kid named Webb? Melanie Webb?'

The woman thought, then shook her head.

'Just thought you might,' the editor said. 'Probably this nag isn't the show type anyway.' He glanced at his notes. 'Stallion. Palomino. Well – thanks anyway, Connie.'

'Stallion?' said the woman, recollection stirring. 'Webb?' She snapped her fingers. 'Star-Wanderer! Good heavens, what's that magnificent creature been up to?'

'Tell you later,' the editor said. 'You wouldn't believe it anyway. Right now, go scoop up whatever the library's got on him and the girl, and bring it here.'

At Radio Station KOOO, the 8 a.m. news broadcast was getting under way. 'We'll take you to Washington in just a few moments,' the newscaster was saying, 'for a report on the President's press conference. But first, a tale of youthful courage and devotion from right here in our own backyard. Not very many minutes ago, Walden County sheriff's officers plucked from the Cascade River a few miles below Ebberley a girl, fourteen, and a boy, fifteen. During the wee hours this morning, the sheriff's office reported, this pair of intrepid teenagers managed to overpower two unidentified men who had abducted the young lady's horse in a houseboat. Let me repeat that, ladies and gentlemen — a *horse* in a *houseboat*.

'Names of the youthful vigilantes are being withheld pending verification, but according to information received by the State Highway Patrol, the horse who was the cause of it all is a palomino stallion who answers to the beautiful name of Star-Wanderer . . .'

A blue sedan northbound on U.S. Highway 99 West, ten miles south of Eugene, suddenly bucked and swerved as if an unexpected gust of wind had struck it.

At its wheel a big man involuntarily blurted out a not-very-polite word and then roared, 'Orbit!'

Beside him a small, dark-haired woman clapped both hands to her cheeks and wailed, 'I *knew* we should never have left them alone!'

In the back seat a young woman with a fabulous new *coiffure* by Don Enrique of San Francisco gasped, then quickly leaned forward, forgetting all about the *coiffure*, and gripped her mother's shoulder. 'Don't worry, Mom,' she said reassuringly. 'She's all right! If she wasn't they'd have said so.'

The speedometer needle of the blue sedan moved swiftly and alarmingly upward.

In the houseboat on the river the horse who was the cause of it all stood in the middle of the ugly cabin, swishing his tail in annoyance at a particularly persistent fly, happily unaware of all the events that he had set in motion.

All he knew at the moment was that he was free at last from the loathsome prison that had squeezed and held him for

as long as he could remember, that his stomach – at least for the moment – wasn't hurting for food, that he felt an almost overmastering urge to get out of this odoriferous place and run and run and run. He would have done it, too, no matter what he had to kick out of his way, if it weren't that Melanie was there and wouldn't let him. She kept making sharp, commanding noises that meant he had to stand still, even though he couldn't see any sense in it. The whole thing wasn't quite so irritating, however, because she was busy going over every inch of him, rubbing hard with something soft. She was talking to the one that usually smelled like Baldy but which now smelled something awful. He was just sitting on the deck with his legs stretched out in front. Orbit ballooned himself with air, then let it all go out in one long, exasperated, satisfying snort.

Melanie, who hadn't given any more thought than Orbit had to radio waves and their role in the spreading of news, paused in her grooming operations to stare towards a grimy square of window glass. 'Well,' she said heavily. 'I can be glad of one thing anyway. Mom and Pop aren't having to do a lot of worrying. They won't be home until this afternoon, and the sheriff's man said we ought to be back by about eleven. Everything will look all normal to them, and I can sort of break the news gently.'

Ritchie looked dubious. 'I don't know. I doubt if Katie has just been sitting around keeping quiet all this time.' He was enjoying sitting down for a while in spite of the fact that he had quite recovered from his exhaustion after resting in the rescue-boat. He had also consumed four chocolate bars given him by the boat's owner. After that he had insisted on swimming back to the houseboat to join Melanie.

Every few minutes, he ducked outside for a look round. After the last reconnaissance he said, 'Gosh, Mellie, you ought to see! I feel like an admiral or something. There are five boats beside the tow-boat, and the sheriff's man must have organized them because they're circling round and keeping other boats from coming too close. It's like a convoy – you know, in wartime.'

Melanie heartily wished she could share in Ritchie's excitement, but she simply couldn't. For one thing she was so tired there was a sort of ringing in her ears. For another, during this interval of relative calm she had had time to think, and her thoughts were anything but cheering.

She and Ritchie had saved Orbit, true enough – and that was more important than anything else. Whether he belonged

178

to her or to Mr Bristow, he was safe. They had snatched him from the hands of men who, whatever else they might do to him, would never love him, and that was a victory worth all the danger and fear and exertion. But the cost! The cost was the wiping out of all her sacrifice for Katie's education. She might just as well have been selfish and hypocritical and kept Orbit. The way things were now, she wouldn't have Orbit, and Katie wouldn't have the education.

The cost of the horribly expensive and horribly ruined boat – and she hadn't a doubt in the world that it was up to her to pay for it – would just about cancel out the eighty-five hundred dollars. That is, if Ritchie was right about the boat's value.

With only a very faint hope that he might be wrong, she tossed a question over her shoulder. 'Are you *sure* Mr Bristow's boat was worth that – that awful amount?'

'Sure, I'm sure. It could be even more.' He came round to Orbit's head where she could see him. 'Why?'

She longed to tell him exactly why, simply because misery loves company, but of course she couldn't. 'Oh, nothing,' she said wearily.

He stared at her. 'If you're worrying that we'll have to pay for that boat, forget it.'

She glanced at him scornfully. 'Oh, sure! Steal somebody's boat and smash it all to pieces, and *forget* it! Really, Ritchie, I'd never have thought you'd – '

'Mellie!' Having tried twice to break into this tirade, Ritchie finally achieved it. 'Mellie, I'm trying to tell you – the *insurance* will pay for it!'

Hope flared through Melanie like a flame, then flickered. 'How – how do you know it's insured?'

He answered patiently. 'Nobody owns a boat like that without insuring it. And anyway, on the control panel there's a little metal plate. With printing on it. It says "Insured by Marine Fire and Casualty". *Now* will you relax?'

Having thus unknowingly delivered Melanie from the

dungeon of her private gloom, the admiral went out on deck for another look around.

By ten o'clock the boat landing below the tiny village of Wilby looked as if a celebration were about to take place. Cars began to arrive and people hurried down to the dock to peer up the river where there was nothing to be seen.

One of them gave a startled exclamation when a handsome young woman stepped out of a houseboat and dropped her baby into the river. The woman smiled reassuringly and said, 'Don't be alarmed, I've got plenty more.'

Mrs Ramsay didn't have any more babies, but she did have a guest. Wearing a pair of white shorts, only slightly soiled, the guest was sprawled in the houseboat's only easy chair, long bare legs stretched out in front of her. With her hostess's manicure set beside her, she was busy doing her nails. She *loathed* doing her nails, Katie had told Mrs Ramsay, so she saved the odious task for times of stress and excitement when she couldn't be putting her mind to something important.

'You don't *look* very upset,' had been Mrs Ramsay's comment, to which Katie replied thoughtfully, 'I guess I'm not, really. Not any more, now that I know Melanie's all right. I'm just sort of resigned to any crazy thing that might happen.'

She glanced up as Mrs Ramsay paused in the doorway, looking towards the scene outside. 'What a mob!' Mrs Ramsay observed. She turned to Katie. 'Latest arrival is the press.'

Katie got up and strolled over to the door, waving her right hand to help the clear nail varnish dry. Among the eight or ten cars and pick-ups parked along the road at the top of the bank, the bright white-and-red press car stood out like a finch among crows. Two men were getting out of it, one of them carrying a camera. Suddenly, out of nowhere, a small figure distinguished by large ears materialized in the path of the newspaper men, talking rapidly, and Katie groaned. 'Conrad! I might have known!'

The minutes went by. More people came, asking questions and exchanging misinformation with those who had come ahead of them. Soon a blue-clad patrolman appeared, walking from one group to another, talking to each in a friendly way but with authority in his tone. 'I'm going to have to clear this dock, folks. You can all see just as well from up there on the bank, and the little lady's going to need some peace and quiet to get that horse back on dry land where he belongs. So if you'll all just move on back . . .'

Aboard the flagship, the barefooted admiral came dashing in from another trip to the bridge. 'Mellie!' he called. 'There's something crazy going on! People keep coming down to the banks on both sides of the river – and waving at us!'

'Maybe they haven't got anything better to do.' Melanie was much too busy to be bothered with trifles. Now that the sun was high it was getting hot in the cabin and she was perspiring freely with the effort of trying to comb Orbit's tail with her own pocket comb. Already she had broken four teeth out of it and could hardly wait to get home, not only to Orbit's own stout aluminium comb but also to the bucket of warm sudsy water which he hated but which was the price he had to pay for beauty.

'But they're waving at *us*!' Ritchie said impatiently. 'One little kid yelled, "Yay, Star Wanderer!" '

Melanie brushed aside a lock of hair which looked more in need of attention than Orbit's. 'Oh, fiddle, Ritchie, what an imagination! Orbit, stand *still*.'

'Imagination nothing! I *heard* him.' He stroked his square chin thoughtfully and did his thinking aloud. 'I wonder how they . . . maybe those officers . . . there must have been some kind of an announce – Mellie! There must have been something on the radio! We –'

'Ritchie, would you mind going out and seeing if the saddle's dry yet?'

He stared at her. It hadn't been fifteen minutes since he had plunged into the river yet again at her peremptory request, dragged the waterlogged show saddle aboard from the sub-merged hulk of *Wayfarer*, and set it on the deck to dry out. He grinned and shook his head with only slightly exaggerated wonder. 'If it wasn't dry ten minutes ago, it isn't dry now. It'll take a week, for gosh sake!'

Struck by a sudden thought, Melanie looked dismayed. 'Oh golly, I didn't use my head. Maybe the leather will crack or something if it dries too fast in the sun. Would you mind too much bringing it inside?'

Ritchie's grin grew broader still. 'I've got a better idea. Why don't I just go chew on it for a couple of weeks. You know, like the Eskimo women do with – '

'Oh, hush!' Melanie said, but she had to smile at him.

They regarded each other with a rather loose-jointed fond-ness, for an interval which was interrupted by Orbit, who threw his head up irritably and shifted his weight from one haunch to the other. His action made Melanie feel a little irritable herself. 'He's getting restless,' she said. 'He wants to be *out* of this place – and so do I! Gee, Ritchie, how much longer do you think it will be?'

Ritchie said, 'I'll go take a look ar – ' He never finished his sentence because he had to scramble sideways to avoid being trampled on. Orbit, reacting in his hair-trigger way to a sud-den roar of sound from somewhere outside, had thrown up his head again, this time banging it sharply on the roof, and danced sideways at the same time.

Moving quickly, but not as quickly as she would have if weariness had not been creeping up on her unawares, Melanie jumped to his head and threw an arm round his neck. 'Ho, now! You big scaredy cat – easy!'

Ritchie, looking startled, said, 'Hey! That was a bunch of people yelling!' He vanished through the door, but in a few moments popped back in again, all but inarticulate with ex-citement. 'Mellie, we're almost there! We just rounded the bend above the – and there's cars all over the place, and about a million people, and – '

182

'Oh, no-o-o!' Melanie wailed in real anguish. 'They'll mill around, and yell their heads off, and Orbit'll – I *told* the sheriff that. Oh, why don't those people go *home*!'

Standing alone on the broad paved ramp leading down to the dock as he faced the crowd lining the bank above him, the highway patrolman looked like an actor about to make a curtain speech. Waving his arms for silence, he called out in a strong voice. 'All right, you people. It's been explained to you why we've got to have it quiet while the little lady gets her horse ashore. I'm going to hold you people responsible. Anybody causing a disturbance will be charged with obstructing an officer in the performance of his duty, and that includes you, there, with the camera. The men in the boats out there can handle everything. They don't need any help. So you people stay put – and stay quiet!'

He turned in time to see the boat which had been doing the towing cast loose its rope and move in a gingerly half circle to place its bow against the houseboat's side, ready to push the big clumsy craft to its berth at the dock. He also saw Ritchie emerge from the cabin and lean over the rail to talk to the two men in the boat, nodding his head several times.

The officer might also have seen one of the men hand Ritchie a coil of rope, but at that instant he became aware of voices and a disturbance on the ramp behind him. He swung angrily round in time to see a very large man with a sun-browned face and determined jaw cleave a path through the tightly-packed spectators like a bulldozer through a strand of corn and start down the ramp with a purposeful stride.

On the tiny deck of Mrs Ramsay's houseboat, Katie looked round too, stared with enormous eyes, and clapped both hands over her mouth in the nick of time to smother what started out to be a yell. '*Pop!*'

The officer, himself no midget, stepped directly into the

path of the newcomer. 'Hold it, mister. Maybe you didn't get the word. All spectators are to stay up there on the bank.'

'I'm not a spectator,' said 'Cuddles' Webb with the polite smile of a man who plans to bother nobody, provided they get out of his way. 'I'm the father of the girl with the horse.' He started forward again as if certain the officer would get out of his way.

The officer didn't. 'My orders,' he said, 'are to keep everybody off this dock. That's what I'm going to do.'

'Orders!' Pop glared – a short-range sort of glare, because his face was only about a foot away from the policeman's. '*Whose* orders?'

The patrolman was glaring too, but his glare was touched up now with a hint of a smile. 'Your daughter's, sir.'

As Katie put it later, 'You could *hear* Pop's muscles relax. They were *audible*.'

To the patrolman all he said was, 'Got any daughters yourself?'

'Two.' The officer was doing considerable relaxing on his own behalf.

'Heaven help you,' Pop said, grinning suddenly and turning. 'I'll go back up there and behave.'

Seated in the white-and-red press car, the young reporter named Dawes was happily making the most of the veritable gold mine of information he had found. The gold mine's name was Conrad Wemmer, and the reporter was taking notes as fast as he could write. 'She trained him to live right in the house,' Conrad was saying, among a great many other things. 'He eats at the table, right with the family; I've seen him do it. And Ritchie Penfield, well, him and Melanie you might say they been going together practically since they were . . .'

Ritchie stuck his head in the cabin door. 'It'll be just a minute, now, Mellie. Be ready for a kind of jar when we hit the dock.'

Melanie nodded and spread her feet a little to brace herself as she stood by Orbit's left shoulder, and took a still firmer grip on the reins. Orbit now was wearing the show bridle which – half a lifetime ago, it seemed to Melanie – had been the weapon that saved her, and he was tongueing the bit nervously, rattling it against his teeth. He would have seemed calmed enough to anyone else, but she knew he wasn't. It seemed as if she could feel through the reins the strange electric vibrations he gave off when he was wound up tight inside.

She was aware of that choking dryness in her throat that always came when she was about to take him into the show ring.

'And Mellie,' Ritchie said, 'a guy's going to help me get this door open farther. I just can't budge it by myself. But he's going to be careful not to do anything sudden.'

He stepped away from the door but appeared again almost at once. 'One more thing. The deck here isn't going to quite match the dock. It'll be maybe three feet higher. Can he step down, or shall we get some boards and – '

She shook her head. 'He'll jump.' The instant she said it she wondered if something had gone wrong with her mind. She didn't really know whether he would jump or not.

For a place where a hundred or more people were gathered on a bright June day, the bank above the boat landing was unnaturally quiet as the strip of dark water between the weatherworn planking of the dock and the square stern of the old houseboat grew narrower and narrower. There were rustlings of whispered conversations. A child piped up. 'Mommy, you said there'd be a *horse*. I don't see any ho – ' The child was instantly shushed and only whispers and mutterings were to be heard.

One of the mutterers was Mom, who was standing between Pop and Diane at the very edge of the bank. 'This whole thing is absolutely mad,' she was saying, in a rattle-brained way that wasn't at all like her. 'You'd think Mellie was coming back from the *moon*. It's so funny I ought to be laughing. So why do I want to cry?'

'Because you're hysterical,' said Pop, who always sounded cross when he was stirred up.

A sort of collective grunt of satisfaction went up from the crowd. The old houseboat had come to rest against the dock with a muffled thud and Ritchie had leaped ashore with a rope, his bare feet soundless on the weathered planking.

A man from one of the boats joined him in mooring the houseboat securely. Next they quickly dismantled the removable section of railing opposite the big door and laid it aside. Then, while the crowd watched in breathless silence, they put their shoulders to the big sliding door that hung slightly askew on its rusty track, and heaved.

At first nothing happened. The door resisted. The boy and the man got a new grip on the deck with their feet, braced themselves, and heaved again.

The door moved back with a teeth-chilling screech of metal. The opening widened – two feet – three feet – four. And then there was an explosion of sound and motion. A high, thin, gasping wail went up from the crowd.

There was a thunderous stamping and clattering of hoofs against the wood and a great eye-rolling, head-tossing apparition of a horse came lunging out on to the tiny deck, thrusting ahead of him the slight, frantically dancing figure of a dark-haired girl in blue jeans and a dirty, dishevelled white shirt.

Orbit had lost his head as disgracefully as a six-month colt. The head-splitting screech of the door, the flood of brilliant sunlight into his gloomy prison, and a confused impression of masses of human beings – all these had erased from his mind in one swift stroke all the lessons of discipline he had ever learned, and he lunged towards freedom.

Melanie, for once, had been caught by surprise. And it was her own fault. Startled herself by the horrible noise the door made, she had looked quickly over her shoulder instead of keeping her eyes on Orbit where they belonged. Worse still, she must have let her hand relax its grip on the reins, permitting him to feel her inattention.

Then everything happened so fast that she felt as if a whirlwind had snatched her into its spinning vortex. The reins slid upwards through her hand, Orbit's great chest slammed into her and she found herself being hurled irresistibly backwards. Her feet and legs moved in a crazy, leaping dance, impelled by the instinct of self-preservation. If she allowed one of those charging hoofs to crunch down on her foot, or a pistoning knee to smash into her abdomen, the result would be broken bones, or worse. Moreover, she was being rushed backwards towards a drop-off which she couldn't possibly see until she had already fallen over it, and when she fell . . .

Out of the middle of the whirlwind – actually out of the middle of Melanie herself – came salvation. The form it took was anger. Hot and cold at the same instant, it was a bitter, all-encompassing sense of outrage – at Orbit for doing this wild, undisciplined, humiliating thing to her, and at herself for letting him get away with it. She didn't think, she simply acted. Recovering her grip on the reins as quickly as she had lost it, she jerked down with all the strength of one arm, and brought the other hand up and round, palm outward, dealing him a stinging slap across the tender tip of his nose. Her voice rang out, clear and compelling in the stunned silence all around.

'Ho! Ho, now! Orbit, how *dare* you!'

Orbit's rush faltered all but imperceptibly. Through the reins, almost through the air, she could feel the shock of the slap and the sound of the shouted command get through to his brain. Once more she repeated the command: 'Ho!' making of it by some miracle the calm, forceful, impossible-to-ignore sound he was accustomed to. At the same time, though still staggering backwards, she planted her feet on the deck as solidly as furious determination could plant them and jammed the point of her shoulder into his chest, never letting up for an instant on the down-and-towards-him tension on the reins.

In a moment it was all over. Still stunned, the watchers on the bank saw the big stallion's lunge come to a halt while his young mistress teetered on the very lip of the drop-off between deck and dock. The next moment, to their collective amazement they saw her take a new grip on the reins with one hand and rap him sharply on the chest with the knuckles of the other, stepping forward at the same time. This time her voice was lower, but still clearly audible. 'Back! Back!'

Two houseboats away, Katie, who had been standing frozen with terror by the railing beside Mrs Ramsay, put both hands to her cheeks and murmured weakly, 'No! I can't *stand* it. She's going to make him go back and do it *right*!'

Melanie lowered her voice, not because of her audience – she had completely forgotten that she had one – but because she knew she had Orbit's full attention now and there was no more need for loud noises. 'Back!' she said. 'You're a disgrace and you know it. Back! Forgot you were a gentleman, didn't you? Back!'

Orbit, ears flat to his head, hating every step of it, backed. He backed through the opening, hoofs thudding hollowly on the boards, backed into the prison he thought he had escaped forever, backed because anything in the world was better than hearing her speak to him in this cold and frightening way.

In the middle of the cabin Melanie halted him abruptly, dropped the reins to the floor and stood looking up at him, fixing his eyes sternly with hers. For a breathless, horrible moment she thought she might keel over in a faint. For the first time she was aware of the bone-weariness that came of hour after long hour of sleeplessness, hunger, emotional stress, and violent exertion. With a vast effort she made her legs behave and her voice sound stronger than it wanted to. 'You think I like this awful place any better than you do? You think *I* didn't want to run out of here screaming like a big baby? Do you think I'd have tried to knock *you* down and trample on . . .'

Her lecture was interrupted by a sound from the doorway,

then Ritchie's strained voice. 'Mellie, for gosh sakes why don't you – '

She silenced him with a violent shake of her head and went on with her scolding. 'Now you're going to stand right there until I tell you to move. Understand?' With that she turned her back on him and started strolling towards the door with feigned unconcern.

It was a stroll that went on for exactly two steps before she halted, frozen with dismay. Those people! The whole county was out there, and they were all looking straight at her! Now she wished she could faint, or had already done so, or better still, simply die on the spot. She knew what they must be thinking, that she was making a grandstand play out of disciplining Orbit. It was nightmarishly unfair.

Her desperate glance encountered Ritchie's as he stood by the door. He said nothing, but his expression was more eloquent than words: Get him out of here. Get him on shore and forget about the discipline.

She longed intensely to do exactly that. Just get out of here and away from all those sneering, misunderstanding people. Forget the discipline. What did it matter?

But it did matter. It mattered terribly, and not just as discipline for its own sake. Orbit out of control, Orbit on a lawless rampage in a strange place crowded with people, would be scarcely less dangerous than a small boy loose on a city street in a high-powered car. If he were allowed to rush off this hateful boat in a panic there was no telling what injury he might do, to the people and to himself as well. No. He *had* to be controlled, had to be brought back to the point at which his only concern in life was to do exactly as he was told.

While the crowd seemed to draw in its breath, she turned back to Orbit and stood silently in front of him while she made herself count to twenty-five. Then she said calmly, 'All right now, are you ready to go to work?'

Trembling slightly, but fully alert, his great dark eyes

watching every move she made, Orbit shook his head in an emphatic negative.

'Then do it anyway.' She gathered up the reins with one decisive movement and spoke softly. 'Hup!'

This time he walked through the door as a gentleman should, and stood like a golden statue when she halted him with a softly-spoken word in the middle of the tiny sun-drenched deck. There she dropped the reins again and stood back, doing her best to close her eyes, ears, and thoughts to the silent crowd above her. 'Orbit,' she said. 'Stretch!'

Eyeing her watchfully, he gave a gentle snort and hesitated just long enough to prove he had a mind of his own, then stepped neatly into the stretch position and held it while she walking leisurely all round him. There was a strange ringing feeling in her head brought on by the impossible effort of pretending she was all alone while she stood there counting senseless numbers.

This time she stopped at twenty, unable to stand another second of it, and said, 'Close up!'

He closed up all too eagerly and she let him stand there another two or three seconds – just long enough to make him wonder if he might perhaps have to do it again. Then she let her face relax at last into a smile, tossed the reins up on his withers, and threw her arms round his neck in a brief hug.

Ducking under his chin to get to his left side, she grabbed a handful of the short hairs at the base of his mane and started to vault to his back. The vault turned into an ignominious scramble, like a small child climbing aboard a fat pony. There simply wasn't any vault left in her legs. Neither, she quickly found out, was there much grip left in her knees, but she gripped them anyway, for what they were worth, and gathered the reins into her left hand. This was going to look more stagey than anything she had done, but she couldn't help it. She didn't know how to jump a horse except from his back and was too tired to figure out another way. It wasn't much of a jump, of course, but it was a different kind of jump. Orbit was used to jumping over things, not down from things, and of course he had never in his life jumped off a houseboat – and for all she knew he might take it into his head that a wooden deck was a thing of deadly peril.

She didn't hesitate, for hesitation would be fatal. Orbit always knew when she was uncertain almost as soon as she knew it herself. She shook slack into the reins, leaned forward, and with a tremendous effort injected the proper note of excitement into her voice as she gave him her own, private jumping command. 'Take it, boy! *Take* it!'

The old deck planking boomed like an out-of-tune kettle-drum as Orbit instantly went into a shuffling little dance, poising his hind feet under him for the jump. The powerful muscles rippled, bunched, tensed. Melanie, through an odd, dreamy sort of fog, heard him suck a vast breath of air – and then he leapt. It was a leap that would have done justice to a steeplechase jumper. He soared above the boards of the dock, coming within a foot or so of clearing it altogether. And he landed with his heart set on going, and going fast. Melanie knew the instant the whip, snap and jar of the jump itself was over that he was going to be hard to hold.

Weary though she was, however, she held him. It was a brief battle but lively, consisting on Melanie's part of a lot of barely perceptible but strenuous movements of her hands on the reins, and on Orbit's of a series of grand opera hoof thunderings, head tossings and curvettings.

Then at last he stood motionless, his head high, his magnificent neck arched with excitement, filled with the wild urge to run, with the joy of finding himself on solid ground again.

For a moment there was no sound at all, and with an unconscious movement Melanie wiped her wrist across her eyes, trying to clear away a misty film that had somehow got in front of them. The crowd lining the bank chose the same moment to let go of its restraint, and the roar that went up caught Melanie by surprise. She had actually succeeded in forgetting during those few tense moments that there was anyone in the world but her and Orbit.

Startled, she curbed Orbit automatically and threw a frowning glance of annoyance at the crowd just exactly in time to have it recorded on film by the *Oregon Daily* photographer.

She didn't even notice the photographer, in whom she hadn't the slightest interest. She had only one thought now: to get out of here, to get away from these silly yelling people, to get home. When Ritchie suddenly appeared beside Orbit, apparently from nowhere, she stared at him stupidly. Her brain didn't seem to be functioning very well.

Ritchie looked up at her anxiously. 'Mellie, you all right?'

'Why shouldn't I be?' she said rather crossly. 'I'm going home now. We'll – we'll get together later.' She gave Orbit a little rein and he promptly started forward, stepping with dainty disdain, as if walking on something that disgusted him. Ritchie trotted along beside, looking up at her nervously now and then.

As they started up the steep ramp, Melanie mechanically leaned forward to help Orbit climb. She was aware of a lot of commotion above her. The crowd, surging in from both sides, was trying to pack itself solid on the ramp for a closer look, and the patrolman, whose control over them was slipping fast, was striding around motioning, commanding, threatening, shoving.

She considered, in a dull sort of way, what to do if the crowd wouldn't make way for her. She could make Orbit rear above their heads, of course. That ought to make them scatter. But to work this manoeuvre bareback would take a lot of energy, and she didn't have a lot of energy. Why – oh, why – wouldn't these stupid people just go away and leave her alone?

'Mellie!' Ritchie called urgently. 'Mellie!' She didn't even hear him.

Then she stiffened, raised her hand, staring blindly forward and upward. Rising clear and compelling above the pandemonium rose a single powerful voice. 'Way! Way! Give way, you meat heads! Way for the horse!'

It was a voice that had once been accustomed to making itself heard – and obeyed – above the rattle of machine-gun fire and the blast of mortar shells in battle. The crowd seemed to surge and boil; then it parted in the middle, and there, striding down the ramp towards her, came – it couldn't be – Melanie knew she must be dreaming – but it was! It was!

'Pop!' she called, her voice weak and thin and childishly piping. 'Oh, Pop!' On one side of her, Ritchie leapt for Orbit's bridle, and on the other Pop reached out his arms and caught her as she fell.

Chapter 19

WHEN the world began to return to Melanie it did so with a strange chorus of buzzing, echoing, underwater sounds. Among them somewhere was Pop's voice, and the feel of his arms round her was too familiar a thing to remain unreal for long. When she could make out his words at last they resolved themselves into, 'You're all right, honey, and so's Orbit.' She started to smile sleepily, because things weren't altogether real yet; but instead she gave a convulsive jump and felt Pop's arms tighten. Orbit! She didn't know whether she said the name aloud or merely thought it, but Pop said quickly, 'He's all right. Ritchie's got him. Now you be quiet. He's taking him over to be with Baldy. Hush now.'

Suddenly Mom's face appeared, looking intensely cheerful and as if she had been crying not very long ago.

'Did you have a nice trip?' Melanie said idiotically.

Things went right on being a little idiotic and not quite real for a long time. Pop slid her into the car as gently as a loaf into an oven, and there was Diane, looking as lovely as ever, and everybody started talking at once.

Then they were home, and there was Katie, looking tousled and cheerful and as welcoming as if she had been there all along instead of having raced home in the pick-up. She flourished a spatula in her hand and said, 'Hi. How do you want your eggs?'

'Eggs?' said Melanie.

'Eggs', Katie said. 'I'm going to feed you, bring back the bloom to your pallid cheeks.' She threw a wicked glance at Pop. 'Sergeant Cuddles' orders.'

'Sergeant Cud – ' Pop, who had been guiding Melanie to a chair as tenderly as if she had been ninety-five and made of meringue, looked up, startled. Then he grinned ruefully. 'You little demon! Remind me to wash your mouth out with soap.'

Melanie hadn't the vaguest idea how long the talking went on – and the eating. It seemed as though whenever they weren't talking they were handing her a plate of something, or a bowl of something, or a cup, and saying, 'Here, eat this.' She ate dutifully, and she did feel stronger. But at last everybody started talking in echoes, and the room began to slide out of shape in front of her eyes at intervals.

It was Mom who put an end to it all by getting abruptly to her feet. 'We've all lost our minds. The poor child's dead for sleep. Ben, carry her up to her room.'

Melanie was awake barely enough to insist feebly that she was quite capable of undressing herself while Mom slid her efficiently out of her clothes and into her pyjamas and tucked the sheet round her. Then the world whirled off, taking Time with it and leaving Melanie behind.

Having not the remotest idea what time she went to sleep, there was no way of knowing how long she slept.

When her eyes fluttered open to stay, she found herself – with no feeling of surprise at all – staring straight at Katie, who was curled up in the chair next to the bed, her yellow-gold head bent over a book. She wore a bright blue-and-green print dress and her hair looked neat and newly washed. Melanie lay watching her in silence as her eyes moved swiftly back and forth, back and forth, across the page.

Feeling as if she were intruding on an intimate conversation, Melanie made a discreet little coughing sound and Katie's eyes flicked up. They exchanged a long look and Katie very slowly smiled. Then she said thoughtfully and surprisingly. 'You know, you're lucky. You're going to be a beautiful old lady.'

Melanie sat up, looking sideways at Katie, half suspecting one of her jokes, but really knowing it wasn't.

'I was looking at you a while ago, and wondering what it

was – and then I knew. It's character! You're loaded with character. Even your *bones* have got character.'

Melanie felt an all but irresistible urge to duck her head and twist a lock of her hair. But even if she had, Katie wouldn't have noticed; she was too wrapped up in her discovery. 'By the time you're fifty,' she went on, 'maybe even forty, nobody will look twice at Diane when you're around.'

'By that time who'll care?' Melanie said, mainly because if she didn't say something she'd start wriggling with embarrassment.

'*You* will,' Katie said severely. 'You never stop caring.'

Melanie was always immensely flattered at being allowed to share Katie's serious moods, but they made her a little uneasy, as if she had to live up to something without being quite sure what it was. 'Well,' she said, elevating her knees to huggable level, 'besides wanting to see how beautiful I'm going to be a hundred years from now, how come you're sitting up here with me. Have I been out of my head or something?'

'You,' Katie said severely, 'have been out of your head ever since you took off on that crazy expedition without waking me up. And before that you were out of your head to – to do what – all for me – Ohhhh, *blast*!'

To Melanie's consternation, she saw Katie's eyes fill rapidly as she struggled with that last disjointed sentence, and heard the 'blast' come out in a strangled sob. Then Katie lowered her head to her hands and wept quietly but without restraint.

Melanie leaped out of bed and stood by the chair in an agony of indecision. Weeping was so unlike Katie. She wanted to touch her, put her arms round her, but didn't dare to. 'What *is* it, Katie?' she whispered over and over. 'What's wrong?'

It was only a minute, though it seemed much longer, before Katie looked up, forcing a smile through the tears. 'Nothing's wrong,' she said, still in the strangled voice. 'Everything's *right*. G-get me a handkerchief.'

Melanie flew to a drawer and brought a handkerchief. Katie scrubbed vigorously at her eyes and struggled with words. 'Oh, what a mess I am! What a big, gooey, sloppy *mess*.' She blew her nose resoundingly. 'And I was going to be so *worldly*, and not even hint how I really felt. But no, I had to break down like a big, blubbering – '

'Katie, for heaven's sake what are you *talking* about?' Relief that apparently no tragedy had occurred while she slept turned Melanie's frantic concern to indignation.

Katie got up abruptly, still dabbing at her eyes, and stood looking out the window. Her voice was much calmer, though still strained. 'Pardon my back. If I look at you I'll start bawling again, so – Mellie, I just want you to know I'll never forget what you did, not if I live to be a *thousand*. I know you. I know you'd rather have sold your *soul* than sell Orbit. But you *did* it, and – '

'Katie!' Melanie sat down on the bed abruptly. 'How – how did you find out?'

Her sister still didn't turn round. 'I'll answer that in a minute. But I've got to say this before I lose my nerve. Mellie, I'm not worth what you did. I'm not! But – but just knowing you *think* I am is the greatest thing that ever happened to me.' She paused, then turned and Melanie saw that she was smiling incandescently. 'End of speech. And a stupid one it was. But I'm normal now, and – oh, golly, there's so much to tell you, and all of it so *fiercely* wonderful. Here, you may as well start with this!' She stooped and picked up a newspaper from the floor beside the chair. Thrusting it into Melanie's uncertain hands, she sat down in the chair and watched Melanie expectantly. 'Go on, read it!'

Melanie stared at her for a moment before looking down at the front page of the *Oregon Daily*. Then she gasped and wailed, 'Oh – no!'

The wail was for a number of excellent reasons. There, in black and white and two columns wide, was a straggle-haired creature, just barely recognizable as Melanie Webb. The creature was scowling ferociously straight into the camera, wearing an outfit, which looked as if it had been bought in a jumble sale, and sitting on a horse who looked, treacherously, absolutely magnificent. Across the top of the picture, in large black type, were the words: *Teenage Couple Routs Rustlers On River*. Below that, in smaller type, were the words: Childhood Sweethearts Save Prize Palomino in Fearless Nocturnal Foray.

Melanie re-read the second line in mounting outrage. 'Childhood sweet – ' she spluttered. 'Where in the world did they get – '

'Guess!' said Katie, who was leaning forward, watching every move.

Melanie's mind raced. 'Conrad!'

'Who else? He *grew* to that newspaper man. Like a *barnacle*.' She plucked the paper impatiently away. 'You can read it all later. There are more pictures on the inside, too. But right now I've got to tell you the news that *isn't* in the paper.'

'Wait a minute!' Melanie ran to the mirror. 'Ugh!' she exclaimed, grabbing her hairbrush, 'I look just like that awful picture. And I'm dirty! Why did everybody let me go to bed without taking a bath?'

'*Let* you! The only way we could have kept you awake was to set *fire* to you. Now, will you *listen*?'

Melanie brushed away at her tangled hair and listened.

'Last night,' Katie began, giving every indication of making the most of her story, 'Mr Bristow phoned.'

'Oh, golly!' breathed Melanie.

'He was terribly excited.'

'No wonder.'

Ignoring these interjections, Katie went on. 'I've had to sort of piece it together, from what I heard Pop say, and what he told Mom, and what Mom told me – but don't worry, I've got it straight. Anyway, Mr Bristow heard about the whole thing, up in British Columbia, and he made Pop tell him about six times that you were all right. And then Pop had to go into a lot of stuff about the boat because he was going to pay for it to the last nickel. And that's when the fight began.'

'Fight?' Melanie echoed.

'Well, not a fight, exactly, but they both got pretty warm and talked loud. Mr Bristow said the boat was covered by insurance, so forget about it. And Pop said don't be silly, insurance doesn't cover a boat that's been stolen and destroyed.

'At that point Mr Bristow told Pop that even if the insurance didn't cover it he guessed he could stand the loss because it was for a very noble cause and he wanted Pop to listen to the proposition that was going to solve everything. So he told him about the proposition and Pop proceeded to blow up. He said the proposition was nothing but a – '

'Katie!' Melanie broke in, '*what* proposition?'

'The *television show*! That's what Mr Bristow *is* – remember? – a big television producer. He said your adventure was a natural for one of his shows that has a trick horse in it, and he'd buy the story and pay for it, and – '

'Pay who?'

'You! And that's when Pop really rocketed. He told Mr Bristow that if he had any more bright ideas about making a charity case out of *his* family, he could blinking well get rid of them. So then Mr Bristow said he'd had a feeling Pop was going to be mule-headed and unrealistic, so he'd just have to work something out and see him tomorrow – which is today.'

Katie giggled. 'Pop got wound up again and laid down the law for five minutes before he realized Mr Bristow had hung up.'

She paused and Melanie said, 'Gee, and I slept through all that?'

'That,' said Katie, 'was nothing to what you slept through this morning when Mr Bristow *got* here!'

'Got here?' Melanie said, going back to her echo act.

'Flew to Portland – in a chartered plane.' Katie paused to sigh deliciously, savouring her story. 'While you've been doing the sleeping beauty bit, Mr Bristow has been a very busy man. He got a lawyer out of bed at six this morning and by nine he was out here with everything signed and sealed.'

'Kate-eeee!' Melanie wailed. 'I don't know what you're *talking* about!'

'You will, dear heart, you will!' Katie carolled. She performed a sort of slow-motion porpoise dive which took her from the chair to the middle of the bed, where she lay on her stomach, with her chin propped on her hands.

'As I was saying, he got here about nine, and Mom said, "Why don't you boys hold your committee meeting out in the workshop, where you won't wake anybody up?" So they did – and guess where your big sister was when they got there! Up in the hayloft with her ear *welded* to the floor just above the workshop.

'Pop brought the meeting to order with no ado whatever. "Now look here, Bristow," he said, "I know your motives are best, and I know you wish you had a family like mine, because you told me so, but you've got to get it into your head that I will *not* go for any trumped-up gimmick for helping me give them an education, or whatever it is you're doing." '

Katie snorted. 'You should have heard the noise Mr Bristow made. "Blank-it-to-blank, Webb," he said, "can't you crawl out from under your overstuffed ego? This is a *business* proposition. I buy ideas all the time – and pay through the nose for them. But I make them pay off if they're good. And this one isn't just good, it's terrific! Listen, have you any idea what a show like this one will be worth to me?"

' "No," Pop said, "and furthermore, I don't want any idea. The whole thing's a phoney, and you know it."

'Mr Bristow sighed a sigh that practically rustled the hay up where I was, and he got real calm. "I knew it," he said. "I knew you wouldn't listen to reason, so now I'm going to tell you something. And whether you like it or not there's not one blasted thing you can do about it." '

Katie performed a flailing contortion that brought her to a sitting position on the foot of the bed where she leaned towards Melanie, hugging herself. 'Oh, golly,' she said breathlessly, 'I'm getting to the good part now.'

Melanie felt like sitting down, but the chair seemed a long way off, so she leaned on the dressing-table instead. 'G-go ahead.'

'Still real calm, Mr Bristow said, "Now stop glaring at me and listen. For about an hour now the U.S. National Bank of Portland has been holding in trust for each of your daughters a block of Bristow Productions stock. The income, and the principal, is to be used at the sole discretion of the trustees to meet the girls' educational expenses. What's left, if anything, will become their property on their twenty-fifth birthdays. So there it is, all shipshape and legal. Nobody in the world – including you and me – can touch those shares or the income from them except the bank. Now, go ahead and yell." '

Katie paused and Melanie stared at her with a sort of bemused solemnity until at last she went on. 'I held my breath, Mellie, because everything was so quiet for so long. Then I heard Pop take a couple of steps. There was a thump when he sat down on something. Then he said, so quietly I could hardly hear him, "Why, Luke? Why did you do this?"

'And Mr Bristow said, "You're not going to yell?" He was trying to give it the – you know, the light touch. But Pop wasn't having any. He said, deadly serious, "There's something behind all this that I don't know about, and I want to know. Why did you do this?"

'After that there was an even longer pause. I'd begun to think they weren't even down there any more. Then Mr Bristow said, "I've already told you. Business. That's the plain truth, but – now don't interrupt. But I might not have thought of it at all if it hadn't been for your daughter."

'Pop said, "Melanie." Just like that. A statement, not a question. "I knew it. What did she do?" '

Katie cleared her throat noisily. Apparently noticing that she was still holding the handkerchief, she wiped her nose and went on. 'Mr Bristow said, very quietly and distinctly. "She sold me her horse."

' "She *what*?" Pop made a noise like an explosion, and it

was a good thing for me because I let out some kind of yelp up there in the loft. And then – and then I didn't feel like yelping at all because Mr Bristow said in a sort of flat tone with spaces between all the words, "She sold me her horse for eighty-five hundred dollars so that her sister could go to Columbia University." '

Melanie, already floundering in a quicksand of confusion and painful embarrassment, was nearly done in completely when she saw the tears well up again in Katie's eyes. But Katie rushed on, angrily shaking her head. 'I'm not going to blubber again – I'm *not*! So Pop said, "Did Mellie tell you that?" and Mr Bristow said, "Of course not. I guessed it. I guessed it. And now I've got to think up some way to weasel out of the deal so that she can keep the horse. Only how will I do it? Maybe I'll have to tell her I gambled my money away and can't afford to buy a – " And he rattled on like that, Mellie, until I wondered if he'd suddenly lost his mind or something, and then all at once I *knew* what he was doing as sure as I'd been down there watching. He was covering up, covering up for Pop, giving him a chance to – you know how men are, Mellie. They'd rather admit they'd been out robbing *graves* than admit that anything could make them *cry*.'

The bed groaned as Katie lunged to her feet with an air of triumph. 'There – I did it! I got clear through it without even sobbing bravely. So now you know everything I know and you can stop looking down at the floor and up at the ceiling and every other pointless place you've been looking for the last ten minutes and – ooops, I forgot something important, *vastly* important. You and I are *not supposed to know anything about this*! If we even *hint* that we do, I'll be branded for life as a shameless eavesdropper, which of course I am. Anyway, Mr Bristow made Pop swear a solemn swear not to tell us anything about it until – oh, lordy, Mellie, do you think you can keep a secret until you're *twenty-five*?'

Melanie was considering this awesome responsibility when there was the sound of running feet on the stairs, and Diane appeared smiling in the doorway. 'Mom said she could tell you were awake, Mellie, by the sound of Katie's voice. Can you answer the phone?'

It was Ritchie, and he was wearing, she could tell, a wall-to-wall grin. 'Hi,' he said. 'This is your childhood sweet-heart.'

'Oh, shut up,' she said inelegantly but without rancour. She was floating far too high to be the slightest bit annoyed with anybody. 'How's Orbit?'

'Orbit! Well for gosh sake, couldn't you at least ask how *I* am first?'

'Okay,' Melanie said agreeably. 'How are you?'

'Fine. Mellie, they're not going to throw me in prison after all!'

'OH!' she gasped, conscience-stricken. She had completely forgotten about Ritchie's multitudinous troubles with the law. 'I'm sorry, Richie, I – what happened?'

'Dad took me to see the judge this morning. He said he ought to throw the book at me, but he was afraid he'd get lynched if he did, because I'm a – ' He broke off.

'Because you're a what?' Melanie prompted.

Ritchie chortled. 'A hero! Didn't you know I was a hero?'

She started to reply scornfully, but something made her pause and give a little thought to the matter. Then she said gravely, 'Gee. You know, you are at that!'

'Hah! Some hero! *You* had to rescue me from drowning! But let me tell you what the judge did, Mellie. He put me on probation!'

'What does that mean?'

'Well, for one thing – ' His voice sounded suspiciously as though he were struggling against laughter. 'For one thing, it means if I get in any more trouble – wham – the guillotine! For another, and this is the bad part, I've got to report regularly to the – the person the judge put me in charge of.'

'Well, that doesn't sound so awful,' Melanie said. 'Who is it?'

There was a kind of snorting explosion on the phone, and Ritchie whooped, '*You!*'

Melanie held the phone away from her ear while he went off into a gale of laughter, and a smile slid over her face – as fiendish a smile as any ever achieved by Katie. 'And what are you supposed to do when you report to your – uh – probation officer?'

'Oh, you know, whatever he says,' snorted Ritchie, who was enjoying himself too much to be cautious.

'And if you *don't* do what he says,' she pursued relentlessly, 'he tells the judge about it and – wham – the guillotine?'

'Now wait a minute, Mellie, it's just a –'

'Ritchie,' she said sweetly. 'Please have Orbit over here in thirty minutes – and then grab a bucket. Your first job will be to help me clean him up.'

There was a pause, during which his slow grin was almost audible. Then he said, 'Yes, sir – I mean, yes, *Ma'am*. I'm on my way!'

'And Ritchie! Thank you for everything!'

Melanie floated up the stairs, her bare feet graciously greeting a carpeted step or two along the way. It wasn't easy to go on floating while taking a shower, but she managed it, and emerged in a glow that covered her on the outside as well as filling her on the inside.

Brushing her hair to a dark glow of its own, she got out a clean pair of jeans and was starting to put them on when she paused, smiled a smile that was only a little bit fiendish, and put them back in the drawer. She got out her jodhpurs instead, and put them on. After all, if the judge had put a slave into her hands there was no need for her to soil herself. Anyway, just this once.

For a moment the old, practical, no-nonsense Melanie threatened to take over and spoil everything; but in the nick of time old Mr Wilby, of all people, came to her rescue. His piping voice – and what an incredibly long time it had been since she heard it – came into her mind from nowhere: '. . . You won't always be young and pretty as a picture and full of fancies like you are now . . .'

Guiltily she took a quick, furtive, and defiant look in her mirror before starting down the stairs on her way to the barn. She really *did* look awfully nice in her jodhpurs.

About the author

William Corbin lives in the Williamette Valley of Oregon, where he operates two filbert orchards on his fifty acres of land. He has travelled in England, Europe, Mexico, and Canada, and writes for various magazines. He is married to Eloise Jarvis McGraw (author of *The Golden Goblet*, which is in Puffins) and has two children and two grandchildren.

If you have enjoyed this book and would like
to know about others which we publish, why
not join the Puffin Club? You will receive the
club magazine, *Puffin Post*, four times a year
and a smart badge and membership book. You
will also be able to enter all the competitions.
For details of cost, and an application form,
send a stamped addressed envelope to:

The Puffin Club Dept. A
Penguin Books Limited
Bath Road
Harmondsworth
Middlesex